Tiger, Tiger

Tiger, Tiger
and Other Stories

Jerry Craven

MONGREL EMPIRE PRESS
NORMAN, OKLAHOMA, UNITED STATES OF AMERICA

Norman, Oklahoma
2012

ISBN: 978-0-9851337-0-2
Library of Congress Control Number: 2012934060
Manufactured in the United States of America

Front Cover Painting: Eric Beverly
Back cover Photograph: Sallie Brown

Mongrel Empire Press
Norman, OK
Online Catalogue: www.mongrelempire.org

This publisher is a proud member of

Acknowledgments

I am grateful to some fine writers and editors whose cafeful reading and insightful suggestions helped shape the stories in this book: Jerry Bradley, Terry Dalrymple, Jim Drummond, Andrew Geyer, A. William Hinson, and Jeanetta Mish.

Some stories in this collection have appeared previously in the following journals and anthologies:

CCTE Studies
"The Garden of the Heads" (winner of the Creative Writing Award)
"Changing Zela" (winner of the George Nixon Prize in Fiction)

Concho River Review
"The Leader of the Band"
"Abu Hassan the Wise"
"Canoeing the Hill Country"
"Brenda without Skin"

descant
"Freshwater Pearl"

Texas Short Fiction
"Red Pickup"

Texas Short Fiction III
"The Greatest Name in Baseball"

Texas Soundtrack
"Two Men—Three Shoes"

A. William Hinson wrote the song that inspired "Two Men—Three Shoes." With Hinson's permission I quoted the song's lyrics in the story.

Four stories are extracts from novels that I hope will soon be published: "El Don and the Bandits" comes from *The Wild Part*, and from that novel's sequel, *Women of Thunder*, I took "Talking to Katrina" and "Brother Jones and the Snake." From *The Jungle's Edge* I took "Brenda Without Skin."

Other books by Jerry Craven include

Tickling Catfish, Texas A&M University Press
Snake Mountain, TCU Press
Becoming Others, Vac Poetry
The Big Thicket, Slough Press
Searching for Rama's Spear, Slough Press
Saving a Songbird and Other Stories, Slough Press

For Rosebell
who knew the art
of telling stories

CONTENTS

Tiger, Tiger

Kent had just finished setting up his canvas when he saw the tiger. It stood on an outcropping of rock high enough up the side of the mountain to make it appear tiny, like a child's toy. Kent's first thought was that he would like to paint the big cat.

The tiger and Kent looked at each other, then it moved into the brush, heading down toward the base of the mountain. Kent glanced at his watch. If I were negotiating that steep trail, he thought, it would take me thirty minutes to get down here. How long will it take a tiger?

Maybe, he thought, I would have been wise to accept Aaron's pistol, along with his offer to teach me to use it. But would the pistol stop something as big as that tiger? Kent thought not. Aaron's assault rifle would, but Aaron had gone to the kampong of the jungle people to get the evening meal. He wasn't due back for almost an hour.

A glance at the trees beside the waterfall pool confirmed what Kent suspected: none were climbable. But would that matter, he asked himself. Couldn't tigers climb trees? He looked again for the tiger.

It walked in jerks as if in pain, dragging a rear leg. Kent decided it wouldn't be so difficult to outrun a tiger that old and crippled, and he felt confident he could get back to the kampong before becoming the tiger's next meal.

With regret, he turned from his canvas and portable easel, trying to memorize the scene so he could find it again. It had, after all, taken him and Aaron three days to locate the place. The beauty of the scene made him catch his breath. This is a perfect spot to paint, he affirmed once more. He would place his Madonna there, beside the pool with the waterfall behind her and the wild profusion of jungle green.

As he jogged along the path beside the stream, he remembered that the trail ran across a grassy area into dense secondary jungle growth toward the kampong of the *orang asli*, the little people of the forest. No tiger would venture close to those folk with their blow guns and poisoned darts.

He moved with care, locating a safe spot between roots for each step. The shallow Malaysian soil forced trees to run their roots along the surface of the trail where generations of *orang asli* foot traffic wore away what little dirt the roots once had over them. The jungle floor reminded Kent of a spooky forest scene from an old Disney movie he had seen as a child. What was the movie, he wondered, picking his way among the tangle of roots. *Snow White*?

He imagined telling Aaron about the incident. Aaron would jerk his head in disbelief and stare. "You were not afraid?" he would demand.

"Some," Kent would admit. "But more than anything else, it was an adventure."

He had said something similar the day before, when Aaron was intent upon cursing the Malay soldiers who led them in circles in the jungle, and Aaron gave him that intense, quizzical look so typical of him. Kent once painted a portrait of Aaron with that look on his face. In the painting, Aaron sat at one of the tables in the Sun Wah coffee house in the old Chinatown district of Kuala Lumpur, his hands hovering above the cut gemstones he sold, his Chinese features caught in a look of intense surprise.

"Life is work," Aaron snapped back. He gestured with contempt toward the soldiers. "A fact that those Malay idiots under my command do not realize. They think life is a game, an amusement."

"Life is more than work—in fact, work must be a minor of living."

Aaron gave him a look that said he thought Kent was teasing. "No one but a Malay believes such rot."

"How is it you know all Malays lack a work ethic?"

"I know from watching them. I know from Othar, once my friend and partner in selling gemstones. Othar worked hard when we first went into business, but as soon as he had a few thousand ringgit, he stopped work. I found him giving his day to lazing in a hammock and feeding goldfish. Can you imagine a more frivolous activity than feeding goldfish? Especially doing something so stupid instead of working. Bah. I fired him as a partner, something he never understood. I want nothing more to do with Othar or any other lazy Malay, and yet the government assigns me those monkeys to help police the jungle."

Kent felt awe for Aaron's entrepreneurial fervor, for his working all week as a government soldier, then giving weekends to hawking gemstones along Petaling Street. When did the man ever relax? When did he give himself permission to be alive without forcing time to be productive for him?

Kent and Aaron looked at the soldiers on the trail in front of them. They chattered and jabbed this way and that with their thumbs, each pointing the direction he thought would lead them to the waterfall and the jungle pool. Kent laughed. "They are a bit comical."

"Yes." Aaron scowled. "The three stooges from American movies brought to Malaysia and made into five soldiers. I suppose you could call them comical. But never do they work. They pretend to work, play as if they work. They eat and belch and sleep and scratch themselves. But real, productive work? Never. They are, after all, Malay."

Amused, Kent watched the soldiers rounding their shoulders, turning their palms upward and shrugging at any direction the others pointed as if saying, "I don't know. Do you know? Do you?" And, of course, none of them knew.

"Look at them," Aaron spat in their direction. "They said they could lead us to a waterfall. But not a one of them could point in the direction of the sky during a rainstorm. The fools. All they want is to get back to their homes so they can sleep and play."

"I like to play," Kent ventured. "Painting is a form of play for me."

"You're a rich man, in Malaysia. Your wealth comes from your painting. When you paint, you work, even if you think it's play. But the Malays—bah. They are animals. You are American and rich. You have nothing in common with these Malay monkeys."

Kent had heard plenty such racist remarks from Chinese-Malaysians, though Aaron seemed more extreme in his racism.

The tangle of the roots seemed to get worse. Kent's shirt clung to him, and the utility belt he wore for his art supplies held a hot band of sweat around his middle. A glance at his watch told him he had been jogging only ten minutes.

Aaron had once said there were no tigers in the jungle this close to Kuala Lumpur. He pushed a tray of gemstones across the table to Kent. "Star sapphires," he said. "Only one of them is worth your consideration. Tigers between here and Ghenting? No. The last tiger to come into Kuala Lumpur arrived as a drowned corpse in the Klang River flood of 1934."

Kent picked up a blue sapphire. Aaron had nodded and said, "Like Chinese and most Americans, you have a good eye. That's my best piece."

The utility belt began to chafe, and Kent stopped to loosen it. He climbed a ridge and looked back toward the stream, lifting his binoculars to search for the waterfall. Yes—there it was.

A fast scan of the area around the pool located the tiger. The size of it staggered him. It sniffed something, then batted it with a paw. "My easel."

Kent looked at his watch. Fifteen minutes. The tiger had come off the mountain much faster than he had thought it would. It could catch up with me, he realized. He put his binoculars back into the case strapped to his hip. In doing so, the ring on his hand caught a shaft of sunlight, and Kent paused to look at it. Magic, he thought, as he always did when he saw the six-pointed star dance over the surface of the blue sapphire Aaron had sold him. Magic.

Titanium oxide inclusions, he told himself: that's what makes the star when the sun strikes it. Ah, but the beauty of it. He turned the ring to admire the magic light, then got back to the trail. This time he ran instead of jogging.

As he crossed an open spot and paused to look at his ankles, fearing he had picked up some leeches from the grass, a movement caught his attention, and he looked back.

The tiger paused in the far edge of the clearing.

Kent turned to find the trail. The kampong, he thought, should be just beyond the clearing. But something wasn't right. The clearing should be much smaller. So I took a wrong turn. And there is no trail. No trail. He looked back to see the tiger coming toward him, looking as big as a horse. He turned to run.

Beneath the trees the undergrowth disappeared except for a few plants that could survive on light filtering through the canopy of leaves overhead. Whichever way Kent looked, the jungle appeared the same. He ran as hard as he could, looking for something—anything—that would help him escape the tiger.

Then he saw the cliff.

Sky opened over the ravine. Kent scrambled through bushes to bare rocks and glanced over the edge. Some forty meters below, the stream that had carved the ravine flowed through a strip of vegetation. Kent looked at the undergrowth along the rim beside him.

"Rattan," he said. The rattan thicket sent its branches snaking into the jungle. Kent hurried to the thicket and pulled at a rope of rattan. But it was no use: the strand gave only a little. The tiger came toward him. Its mouth hung open, and it seemed to have lost its limp.

In a panic, Kent seized another strand of rattan and pulled it toward the cliff. He got about one meter of the vine over the edge when he heard the tiger crashing through the rattan thicket.

"Don't break," he commanded as he gripped the vine and scrambled over the face of the cliff. The rattan responded to his weight by unraveling a bit more of its length.

He looked up. The tiger stood above him, jerking its head this way and that, looking for a way to get to him. Kent tightened his grip on the rattan and looked down.

Below, a thin strip of jungle grew along the stream. It looked like grass, but Kent realized with a start that it was trees. One hand slipped on the rattan. He held tight with the other and reached up for a firmer grip. The rattan slipped a bit more, bouncing him against the face of the cliff.

Kent felt about the cliff with his feet, found a slight protrusion of rock, and used it to take some of the weight off his hands. He couldn't stand on the rock, but it did afford some relief. "Aaron, I believe it's time for you to show up," he said, looking at his watch.

The crystal of the watch had shattered, and the minute hand hung out like a thorn. The hour hand had vanished. Kent refocused attention on the vine. A loop in the rattan would help, he decided. It seemed pliable enough, if the loop were large.

Keeping much of his weight on one foot, Kent squatted, clung to the vine with one hand and with the other removed the leather shoelace from one of his hiking boots. Then he drew the rattan vine into a circle, moving with great care so as not to lose his grip on it. Using one hand and his teeth, he tied the rattan to itself, making a loop almost two meters in diameter.

He pulled himself up and sat in the loop. It sagged but held. Kent thought of Aaron again and glanced at his broken watch. He unbuckled the band and threw the dead instrument into the ravine, then inspected the job he had done tying the rattan together. It seemed to be holding well. He heaved a sigh of relief.

The sound caused a flurry of activity from the tiger. It reached toward him, claws extended, and raked the rock above his head. Kent laughed, aware that the sound was thin and strained. "Lost your evening meal, did you?" He took a deep breath and became aware of the smell.

It had been there all along, Kent realized, but he didn't have the leisure to notice. Rotten fruit. Worse than rotten. He looked above him at the trees hanging over the edge of the cliff and muttered a single word: "durian."

The durian stood like a giant among the other trees, and high in its branches hung an abundance of the spiky fruit. Kent had seen them in stalls of the night market in Shah Alam, but he had never had the nerve to try one. Durian smelled so terrible. "Like an outhouse," Aaron had once

5

remarked. "But they taste like heaven." Kent had his doubts about that. Still, he thought one day he might try eating a durian to see if he could get around the smell.

Aaron told him that Malays believed durian to be an aphrodisiac. "They say that when the durian come down," Aaron explained, "the sarongs go up. But of course the Malays are primitive and have all sorts of false ideas. "

The tiger huffed and coughed. Kent laughed again, this time noting that he sounded more normal. He was, after all, safe for the moment—and even comfortable. Sitting on the rattan loop even allowed him free use of his hands.

He looked at the tiger. It had an air of regal disappointment about it, Kent thought, along with a fierce feline determination. It settled on the edge of the cliff, dangling one monstrous paw over the edge and looking at him. Kent looked at the rock cliff beside him.

Run-off from rain had stained the cliff with streaks of brown and gray. In West Texas, Kent thought, we would call that stain "desert varnish." What is it here? Jungle varnish? He took his knife from his belt and scratched the rock. The stain resisted being scraped away.

He pulled a tube of oil paint from his utility belt and squeezed some of it onto his pants, just above the knee, then selected another tube to blend colors. In scrambling over the cliff, he had broken the handles of two brushes protruding from the belt, but that still left him four to work with. He took one of the brushes, blended the paint on his leg, and looked up at the tiger. "I'll immortalize your flashing eye and burning fur on this rock." Kent began applying paint to the cliff face beside him. "Or at lest put you here for as long as the jungle will allow."

With the speed and accuracy of the experienced artist, Kent dabbed paint on the rock. Before long, two tigers looked at him: one from above and one from under his moving brush. Kent pushed back from the cliff, leaning out as far as he could. But he was still too close to the work to see it as he wanted. He turned in the rattan swing to get farther away, and that was when he saw the durian.

It rested on a tiny ledge off to his left, out of reach. No wonder the smell of durian is so strong, he thought. He tried standing on the loop and reaching, but the fruit remained just beyond his fingers.

Kent thought the rattan strong enough to hold up an elephant. Would it take the stress of swinging it a bit? He nudged out from the cliff at an angle and swung toward the durian. His fingers brushed it before he swung away. Close. Another two swings, and I'll have a meal.

He pushed again, harder. This time the arc of his swing took him to the ledge, and he caught the durian in one hand. The spikes on its skin bit into his palms, but he didn't loosen his grip.

As he swung back beyond the painting of the tiger, he felt something give in the rattan, and his loop fell almost a meter. He clutched the durian to his chest and held tight to the rattan. When he looked up, the tiger was standing, looking at him with the curiosity of a house cat.

The rattan life-line had broken loose from something—from other strands of the vine, he decided. But it still held.

No more swinging, he vowed. But it might have been worth the risk to get the fruit. He put the durian into his lap, took the knife from his utility belt, and cut into the fruit.

The smell got worse. But that texture. He pulled out a piece of white pulp and held it to the light. Beautiful. Like a curd of cottage cheese that had the celled texture of a plant. He put it into his mouth. "By God, Aaron was right. Durian is delicious." He took another bite, thinking about how he would tell Aaron of his first taste of durian.

Kent laughed at the thought. The tiger coughed. "What's that, old buddy? Still hungry? Here, have some durian." He threw a piece of the fruit toward the tiger.

The pulp stuck on the tiger's paw. It licked the fruit into its mouth and made two pumps of its jaw before swallowing. Kent laughed. "You liked that, pussycat? Have another piece. I'll share my dinner with you, even if I'm too rude to volunteer to be your dinner."

As he threw another piece of durian to the tiger, Kent saw in his periphery the glint of sun on metal from the rock ledge on the other side of the ravine. He looked across at Aaron staring at him in amazement.

"Aaron. If you would find your way over here, I would gladly share my durian with you."

Aaron unstrapped his assault rifle from his shoulder. "I'll dispatch that tiger for you."

"No. I forbid it. That tiger deserves to live as much as you or I. And look, it's now my friend." Kent threw another piece of durian to the tiger. "We're sharing a meal."

Aaron stared. "On the rock," Aaron pointed. "You painted the tiger?"

"Yes. It's a magnificent tiger, is it not?"

"You play with paint and you feed the beast? You hang between death and death, and you do nothing? You play games just like those Malay animals you hired. You eat and paint and feed the tiger?" Aaron's voice carried the same harsh, racist edge he used when talking about Malays.

7

Kent could see rage coloring his cheeks.

"Yes. Aaron, everyone hangs between death and death. For me," he gestured at the ravine below and the tiger above, "it's just a bit more obvious."

"Are all men from Texas such idiots? Worse than Malay monkeys who would feed goldfish instead of working?" Aaron shouted the words. Kent watched him point his rifle toward the tiger.

"No." Kent raised his voice but was drowned out by the chatter of automatic rifle fire. He looked up to see the tiger jerk upright in surprise. Leaves drifted into the ravine.

Kent looked in astonishment at the cold fury on Aaron's face as the man fired burst after burst into the jungle above the cliff.

The Leader of the Band

Melissa Sue told her Dad that old man Tucker tried to get into the car with her, and her dad got so hot about it that he went looking for Tucker with a pistol. Tucker had come up to Melissa Sue when she was in a car waiting for her pa to get out of the supermarket. I was sitting on the curb, shooting sparrows with my bean-shooter when he done it, so I seen it all.

I never killed a sparrow, but I made them squawk and flutter ever once in a while. They didn't seem to mind much. They always went after the beans like they was grasshoppers. I figured it was a fair enough trade: they served me for targets, and I let them eat the beans I shot at them.

Tucker went stumbling over to the car, mumbling like he always does, only he was looking at Melissa Sue in a kind of weird way, like he was glad to see her, which was strange for Tucker since he didn't ever seem glad to see anybody, except the high school band, of course. And he didn't ever talk to nobody but himself, not since he moved to our neighborhood, and for sure not to me. I was as nice to him as I could be—nicer than I was to our cat, even, and he still always looked right past me when I tried to get him to talk. So when it seemed like he would say something to Melissa Sue, I gave the sparrows a rest and watched.

She went to rolling up her window ninety to nothing and locking all the doors. Melissa Sue is sometimes dumb as hammered cow flop. There was Tucker all set to break a record by talking to somebody in our neighborhood and she goes to acting like that. I guess I shouldn't be so hard on Melissa Sue, though. Tucker was a right ugly sight with his ratty beard and hair and black coat that he had trussed up around him with a hemp rope. His socks leaked out of his boots in five or six spots, not that you could tell real easy on account of the socks being so dirty. The knees to his pants was rubbed partly away from crawling around under the lumberyard, and he had bits of grass and mud sticking to him most all over.

It crossed my mind that Melissa Sue maybe got a whiff of Tucker and

9

that set her to rolling up the windows. He always smelled like a wet dog that just rolled in something dead. But then I saw her go to locking the doors, and that's when I wanted to go after her with my bean shooter.

I seen the rest of what Tucker done, too, and it was nothing like what Melissa Sue told her pa. I should have set him straight when he came out of the store, but how was I to know the whopper she was going to come up with?

I went back to the business of thumping the sparrows around and feeding them with my bean shooter, but my heart wasn't in it anymore. All I could think of was how I missed my chance to hear Tucker talk to somebody besides himself. So I headed home, taking the back alley just in case I might get lucky and catch Tucker crawling under the lumberyard. But he must have been on to me cause I saw nothing of him. Tucker don't like nobody seeing him going in or out of his house. Not that I blame him, considering how fast the Broussard brothers would evict him if they had any suspicion he was living under their place of business.

I scrunched over some in my backyard to take a fast look for Tucker. And just as I figured, old Tucker was under there. He must have gone in from the other side, else there was no way he could have beat me home.

Soon as I got into the house, Aunt Lillian hollered at me to come to the front room. Melissa Sue and her pa was in there. He was all red-faced and sweaty, and Melissa Sue looked real proud of herself.

"Calvin says that old drunk, whatzisname, Tucker, tried to get into the car with Melissa Sue when she was waiting in the parking lot of the store," Aunt Lillian said.

"He ain't an old drunk," I said. "He never drinks nothing but water from our hose."

"Locked him out, though," Melissa Sue said. "So he went to beating on the door and cussing at me. When he saw how he was locked out, he picked up some rocks to bust out the window with."

"I aim to shoot the child-molester," her pa said. And he had a gun, too. I could see it poking out of his belt, under his shirt.

"You'll do nothing of the kind," Aunt Lillian said. "You do, and the law will rack you up in Huntsville, maybe even electrocute you, and then who would look after Melissa Sue?"

"Ain't a jury in Port Arthur or in the whole state of Texas would send me away for shooting him that molested my daughter," Calvin said. Melissa Sue liked that kind of talk from her pa, I could tell. But it made me sick.

"Tucker never done nothing like that," I said. "I was right there, and

I seen it all. He never tried to do nothing but talk to her, and she ruined his chance to talk by playing like a scared dog. I seen it all."

"Did too," Melissa Sue said. "Did too. And he was going to bust out the window to get to me, but he musta got scared of pa, so he high-tailed it."

"He never. I seen it all. He never had nothing in mind but talking."

"Now, Larry," Aunt Lillian said, "how could you know what that old derelict had in mind? He tried right hard to get Melissa Sue's door open, to hear her tell it."

"Then you got to hear me tell it, cause I seen it. He just went to talk to her, and she took to winding up the windows. Old Tucker sort of stumbled. Did it on his own shoelaces, and nearly fell—that's why he grabbed the door handle. To keep from failing. When he got steady and seen how Melissa Sue was scared half to death, he went on off."

"I weren't scared. And he went to picking up rocks to bust out the window."

"You was plenty scared," Calvin said. "When I got out to the car, Miss Lillian, she was plumb white, and the little bugger was trembling all over."

"That old man does go around with his laces flopping all over the place. I always wondered how come he never fell from it," Aunt Lillian said.

"Bottle caps," I said. "Tucker found some bottle caps when he turned away from the car, and he picked them up. I seen him. I was right there. Tucker collects bottle caps."

"Nobody collects bottle caps, and it was rocks he picked up, rocks to throw into the window so he could get at me."

"Was Larry there?" Calvin asked Melissa Sue.

"Maybe."

"That old man for a fact collects bottle caps," Aunt Lillian said. "He took to leaving some of them on our back porch. Never seen anything like it. Loose shoe laces and bottle caps—don't that beat all?"

"Give me a better answer than that, Melissa Sue. Did you see Larry there?"

"Maybe."

"Not maybe. You saw him or you didn't. Which was it?" Her pa was starting to get a little hot, this time at Melissa Sue, and she backed off some.

"I guess. Yes. Larry was hanging around the store, killing birds. But that old man, he tried—"

"I never killed one bird. Never."

11

"You take her home and fix her some hot mint tea and get her under a Vicks tent," Aunt Lillian said. Aunt Lillian thinks ever ailment in the world can be fixed up with mint tea and a Vicks tent. That and cod liver oil. She is all the time trying to pour cod liver oil into me when she thinks I'm not acting right.

"You seen him pick up bottle caps, Larry?"

"Yessir. Lotsa times. And he got some right after he found he couldn't talk to Melissa Sue. Tucker, he might be a little crazy, and for a fact he don't like to bathe, and he is a mite scary-looking, specially to somebody like Melissa Sue. But he wouldn't hurt nobody. He—"

"And if the Vicks tent don't get her to feeling better, you give her some cod liver oil, first thing in the morning."

By that time I guess Calvin got calmed down some, and maybe he was remembering how his daughter made it a habit of letting her imagination run wild. Melissa Sue clammed up. I figured it was because she was afraid her pa would take Aunt Lillian's medical advice and come at her with the cod liver oil.

When Calvin and Melissa Sue left, he was muttering about how somebody ought to talk to that crazy old man about not going around scaring little girls. I took that to be a sign that he was going to leave off hunting for Tucker with a pistol. Right as they walked out the door, Melissa Sue stopped just long enough to shoot me a mean look. I guessed she was telling me to forget walking to school with her for a while. And that was just fine with me cause I was ticked off at her for getting her pa so fired up about Tucker.

Her pa wasn't a bad sort, though. He might fly off the handle sometimes, but I figured deep down inside he was as nice a guy as the rest of my neighbors.

After supper that evening I spooned up some black-eyed peas with a few chunks of ham hocks into a pan, added the left-over smothered cabbage that Aunt Lillian was about to throw out anyhow, along with a couple of biscuits, set a lid on the pan to keep Hannibal from getting at the food, and took it to the back porch. Aunt Lillian groused some about me feeding that old bum, but she didn't mean it. Hannibal went to pawing around on the pot soon as I set it down, then lost interest soon, same as always. Cats are smart enough not to worry with things that are beyond them, and old Hannibal never could do much with getting into that pan. Not that she tried all that hard, what with her own food there beside it, available for no work at all. I figured that spread would be worth three bottle caps and a plastic button to Tucker on account of how much he went for black-eyed peas and cabbage.

But I was wrong. The next morning, inside the scrub-bed-out pan was four bottle caps and a solid brass button. Tucker went for that food in a bigger way than I had thought. It must have been the ham hocks.

One time I left him a chef salad on account of that's what we had for supper, and I don't ever cook special for Tucker. I thought if it was good enough for us, it was good enough for Tucker. He thought different on the matter, though. He never touched what was in the pan that night, and he left one rusty bottle cap on top of the pan. That was his way of saying he looked inside and found it not worth eating and not worth paying for. Sort of like leaving one penny for a tip just to let the waiter know you didn't forget about tipping but that you didn't think he was worth more than one cent. And he done something else to let me know what he thought of the salad. He went back to eating Hannibal's dried cat food. Left the bowl empty, except for a couple of Pepsi caps to let me know where the cat food went.

About the time that Tucker began living in our neighborhood—before I found out about his spot under the lumberyard—I just happened to look out my window, which is upstairs, and saw Tucker eating Hannibal's food. Next day I told Aunt Lillian about that. I waited until she was busy with the ironing so she would listen. Sometimes she don't listen to me much, like when she is reading a book. She will just hum and say, "Yeah, sure," not meaning it at all but just saying something to cover up for not listening.

"How come he would eat that stuff?" I asked. "It's plumb horrible."

"Horrible, is it? How would you know that?"

"Tried it. Tried it this morning when I was thinking on him sitting there last night eating half a bowl of it. I can see a body trying it like I done out of curiosity. But he ate all there was."

"That old man was hungry, Larry. Poor old man." Aunt Lillian sniffed a couple of times like she was real sad, then went off to refill her Coke bottle that she used to sprinkle the clothes with.

So I took to sharing our food with Tucker, leaving on the porch some of what we had for supper, and he took to paying for it with bottle caps and buttons. Aunt Lillian said I ought not take the worthless junk he left, that I made it easier for him to believe that he was paying his way instead of living on hand-outs. "A man that is a bum ought to at least be man enough to admit that he is," she said.

But I was of a different mind on the matter. He had to scrounge around a bunch for those bottle caps and buttons. I watched him. He could go all day and not collect many, not the way he went about it. And the buttons was harder. He gathered them under clothes lines in the neighborhood, picking up buttons that worked loose from wear and from washing and then got beat off when the wind blew the clothes around. Once I seen him pull a button off a shirt, but it was real loose and just hanging there by a thread. It would have fell anyway, sooner or later, so it wasn't like old Tucker was stealing it. He was just helping it in its natural progress going from being loose to falling on the ground. Anyway, Tucker worked hard for his bottle caps and buttons, so they was worth something, to him, anyway. Which is the same thing as them being valuable. So I took his pay and felt it was a fair deal. Four bottle caps and a solid brass button might be half a day's work for Tucker, and who can say that half a day isn't a fair price to pay for a good meal?

Aunt Lillian crabbed some ever time I took food out for Tucker. "You're just like Jolsen," she told me the first evening I gathered food for him. "He was always dragging home starving dogs and one-eyed cats and crippled frogs. Never seen nothing like it. Picked up birds that blew out of a nest in the pecan tree, he did, and went to shoving food down their throats with an eye dropper. Made them live, too, until one of his stray dogs that he brought home all mangy and half dead ate them. Jolsen never even whupped the dog. Said it was the dog's nature, that he was at fault for leaving them where the dog could get at them. Soft hearted to the point of being soft headed. And you're following in his footsteps with feeding that old man."

I took it as a compliment, being compared to my older brother Jolsen, who was off in the Navy. But I think Aunt Lillian was just blowing hot air, cause she never told me not to feed the old man, and after a few days, I noticed she was cooking enough for me to have plenty left-overs to take out. Like as not if I hadn't gone to feeding Tucker, Aunt Lillian would have. Anybody in our neighborhood would have done the same thing, or so I believed.

I took the four bottle caps and the brass button and scattered them about so Tucker could find them again. The caps went to the alley, and I chunked the brass button into old man Glenn's yard, right under his clothes line where Tucker goes foraging.

Just in case Melissa Sue was over being mad at me, I walked to school by way of her house. But she didn't wait for me like usual. So I went to Elizabeth Street School for a hard day in D-minus Daniel's class, where I worked some and fooled off a lot and mostly forgot about Melissa Sue and Tucker.

14

After school, the sky got gray like it was going to haul off and rain so the band couldn't march. But it stayed dry, and I went to the high school drill field right across from my house and waited for the band. Jolsen was leader of the band before he run away and joined the Navy. Used to, I always watched because he was out there, and since he left, I get over there most every day and pretend it's still him with the baton and the whistle, making the band play in time and telling them how to march.

Tucker was there, same as always. Or same as always since some weeks back when he took up residence under the lumberyard. I stood on the top of the bleachers to get a better view of the patterns the band made. Tucker hobbled around on the edge of the field, just ahead of the band. He carried a twig, a gnarled-up dead-looking thing that might have been a hackberry branch in a past life, and he took to pretending to lead the band soon as it started playing. I knew if I got up close he would be making crazy sounds like "Bah bah bah boom bah bah tweeet tweeet." And he would strut some to look like the drum major, only he always looked more like a crazy old man making fun of the drum major.

Which is what I thought he was doing until I talked it over with Aunt Lillian. It teed me off, thinking Tucker was making fun of the leader of the band, especially since I always pretended that it was still my brother Jolsen out there with the baton, the funny striped pants, the vest covered with brass buttons, and the tall hat. From on top of the bleachers, there was no way to tell one drum major from another since the new guy wore the same kind of uniform Jolsen did when he ran things on the band field. Teed me off good and proper, thinking Tucker was maybe making fun of Jolsen.

But Aunt Lillian said like as not old Tucker didn't think he was making fun of anybody. She said he was pretending to be drum major, probably because it made him feel like something besides an old derelict, and he could be happy some.

Seen like that, I forgave Tucker. And after a few days it seemed like a natural part of band practice, for me anyway, to have him out there with his sad-looking twig, making noise like a tuba and the drum major's whistle.

I watched the band some, thinking of Jolsen. And Tucker some, wondering how come an old man like that would want to be in a band full of young folk. Then the rain came, slow at first, but enough to scatter the band. Tucker went "Tweet, peetweet, tweet," angry-like, and stomped out on the field, jerking the hackberry twig around and making some mean faces. But nobody paid him any mind; they just run for cover because the

15

rain started pelting down. I took off for home, but I only ran a little because I saw this rain was a real toad-choker, and I would get soaked no matter what. Aunt Lillian would have a cow when she saw me, and like as not I would have to face a spoon full of cod liver oil to ward off a cold. The thought of the cod liver oil slowed me even more.

Then I got to watching Tucker. He still had a real mad on, but even he must have got to thinking how much better it would be to get somewhere dry. He worked out the mad by breaking the hackberry stick across his knee, and then he threw it down and jumped on the pieces before heading for the fence at the edge of the field.

I had gone down the block to get to the gate, but Tucker went straight toward the lumberyard, like the fence wasn't even there. When he got to it, he went to climbing. I stopped cold and stood there with rain beating puddles all over the place, soaking me something awful, and watched old Tucker get to the top of the chain-link fence like it was nothing. When he set his hands on the top to jump over, I could see what was coming.

The wire tore into the center of both his hands, sending blood down the fence with the rain. Tucker flipped himself over and landed on his knees in the mud. He caught himself from falling on his face, but to do that he had to stick his hands into mud. When he stood up, he looked sort of dizzy. I could see the mud on his hands turning pink.

When Tucker slogged through the ditch and up on the road, right across from me, it was raining like the sky just opened up. He took a quick look both ways, but he come on out in the street anyway.

And that's when the car got him. It was a big, cream colored Buick, one of those old ones built with metal thick as a manhole cover, and it clipped Tucker in the side with a mirror that stuck out too far, then bumped him hard on the door. He didn't fall, but he spun around right fierce, and in spite of the noise of the car and the rain, I heard Tucker grunt.

I ran to him, and he let me steady him some. That Buick never stopped, not that it mattered to Tucker. He headed out into the street. I looked both ways and went with him, trying to hold him up. He hunkered over a bunch and held his side with hands that was dirty with bloody mud. "You just come on to our house," I told him. "Me and Aunt Lillian will get you dry and—"

But he wasn't listening, so I shut up. He was mumbling. It was hard to make out, but some of it was plain: "—car broke my leg again," he said. "Never was no good, but I tried, I tried."

We made it across the road, and I thought we was heading to my house. But Tucker had other plans and pulled off between the house and the lumberyard. There was nothing I could do to stop him, so I went along to see if I could keep him from falling down before he got to a place where he could crawl under.

At the edge of the lumberyard I kind of lowered him to the ground. He kept muttering, so there was no use in me trying to talk him into coming inside for help. The overhang dumped a steady wall of water off the building, like a white sheet, and we had to be in it while Tucker struggled to crawl between a couple of foundation pillars. I went under part way with him, but he paid me no mind.

A few days before, I had crawled under with a flashlight to check out how he lived under there. About thirty feet under I found some strips of cardboard that he hauled in for a floor. There was a couple of Coke bottles sitting on a brick, one full of water, the other with a few swallows left in it, along with a bunch of cloudy-looking backwash. By the bottles was a mirror in a metal case with the glass busted all to flinders. He had a frying pan under there, old and rusty on the outside with about a handful of dried cat food in it. And there was ants and a couple of roaches in there, too, working on the cat food. My guess was that he had no idea about the critters that shared the food with him on account of the dark way under that building.

Tucker got just a few feet under when he stopped, and I could tell he was as far as he wanted to be for the night. So I got out of there, bathing in the run-off from the roof to keep Aunt Lillian from passing out when she saw me covered with mud. The rain was starting to slack off some, but there was plenty of water still falling off the roof, and I got cleaner than any tub bath could get me.

By the time I got dried off in the house, the rain had stopped. Aunt Lillian nearly had a conniption fit over how wet I was, but she hushed when I told her about Tucker. She dished up a bunch of mustard greens that she was cooking, dumped in some vinegar to make the pot likker good, and threw in some sow belly. "You give this to that old man," she said. "And some biscuits, too." She buttered up some biscuits and stuck them in with the greens.

I set the food on the porch, then bent over by the lumber yard.

"Tucker, there's hot greens and vinegar and sow belly and biscuits over here. You come get it, hear?"

He just laid there, and I got to feeling silly for calling him Tucker like that was his real name. Truth is, nobody knew his name. I just called him that on account of seeing him in my backyard one day washing his feet in the rusty frying pan he kept under the lumberyard. Seeing that put me in mind of a song Jolsen used to sing about a good old man named Tucker who washed his face in a frying pan, combed up his hair with a wagon wheel and then died with a toothache in his heel.

He was still there, breathing heavy and mumbling, but he never answered me. I got down on one knee and stuck my head under the building. That was when I heard him crying. Not loud like Melissa Sue cries, but low and quiet, like Jolsen did the night his girl friend told him not to come to her house again. Jolsen never even went back to school after that night, and he went and joined up with the Navy the next day.

"Don't you go to carrying on like that," I said. "Come on out and have a hot meal, okay?" He sort of twitched some and whimpered a couple of times instead of answering. But I got the feeling he was listening to me. "You come on now. Make you feel better to eat. And I got a present for you, okay?" That last part I just added on the spur of the moment, not having anything in mind to give him. I wanted to help, same as I wanted to help my brother Jolsen that other night but couldn't come up with a way to do it.

Back in the house I went to rummaging around my room, looking for something to leave out for Tucker to cheer him up. But what could I offer that meant anything to someone like him? Bottle caps? I for sure didn't keep any around. Then I went into Jolsen's room to see if anything in there gave me an idea about what to do. When I looked in Jolsen's closet the ideas started coming.

Hanging on the first hanger was his drum major outfit with brass buttons all over the vest. First I considered cutting all the buttons off, cause Tucker would go for that brass in a big way. Then it came to me slow-like, and I stood there, caught by how right the idea was, hardly breathing with excitement over it.

I took the whole outfit—the pants with the stripe, the top with all the brass buttons, the baton, the white shoes—and put them out on the back porch on a towel to keep everything off the wet steps. Then I ran over and told Tucker, "You'll find it on the porch by your supper. Hope you like it."

That night when I went to bed, I felt better than I had since before Jolsen left, and the first thing I did the next morning was look out on the porch. The towel was still there, rumpled up in a heap. But the uniform was gone.

I didn't tell Aunt Lillian about giving Tucker Jolsen's uniform cause I was scared she wouldn't see the matter the same way I did. She knew I done something, though, cause she kept asking why I was smiling so much during breakfast. "You sure you're all right?" she asked for about the thousandth time.

"Great."

"What you been up to? You look like the possum that made off with the sugar bowl."

"Been up to nothing."

"Then you're getting sick from being in the rain last night. Might that be it?"

"Aunt Lillian," I said, "I feel terrific. In fact, I feel more like I do right now than I ever have before." I got that line from Jolsen, and it worked like I wanted it to. She chewed on that idea for long enough to let me grab my books and head for the door.

"When you get home, I'm going to take your temperature, and maybe give you a spoon full of cod—"

I shut the door and headed down the block, wondering if Melissa Sue was over her mad enough to walk to school with me again. Then I saw the ruckus in the corner of the marching field. People milled around, and there was a couple of police cars. Melissa Sue was there, so I went over to find out what was going on.

Her face was all red from excitement, and she started talking before I got up to her. "He done it standing up," she said, "right over there, in the corner of the fence, so he could hang his arms over the top to hold him up. That guy over there told me they had to pry the watchamacallit out of his hand on account of him being all stove up from being dead all night. Rigger morris, the guy said, which is something dead people get when they stay dead too long."

"Slow down, Melissa Sue," I said. "Who are you talking about, and what did he do standing up?"

"He died standing up, that's what. Arms spread out and hanging on the fence. They took him away sos I didn't get to see, but that guy over there told me all about it. Said the crazy old drunk was all broken up here," she touched her side, "like he fell off a roof or something, making him all bleedy inside, so he done it, he died standing up and still holding a whatchamacallit, a baton and wearing the uniform of a drum major—"

"Tucker? You telling me Tucker is dead?" I grabbed her arm and gave her a hard shake.

"Yeah." She jerked away. "Your buddy and friend who tried to bash in Daddy's car to get at me. Dead as a mackerel. And you know what? I'm glad. Glad." She backed away from me.

I wanted to pick up a handful of mud and chunk it right in her face.

19

But I didn't. And all the sudden I didn't care about Melissa Sue and the rest of my neighbors hanging around talking about Tucker like he was nothing, like he was a piece of garbage they found hanging on the fence. All I wanted was to be by myself.

Instead of getting on to school, I went to the lumberyard where Tucker lived, and then on into my backyard so I could sit on the porch and think all this through.

Did he at least enjoy his last supper? I wondered.

But he didn't. When I looked in the pan we left for him, I found the biscuits all sorry-looking and green from soaking up the pot likker. He ate nothing, not even the sow belly. The towel was beside the food, like I noticed earlier. Only I hadn't looked too close, or I would have seen it had dirt and blood on it from Tucker cleaning up before handling the uniform.

Under the towel was a whole paper bag full of bottle caps and buttons.

The Garden of the Heads

Frank stepped through the iron gate and went to the corner of the courtyard, pausing to look at the bullet holes in the faces of the poet and the two communists. Then he noticed a yellowing in the foliage of the flower beds around the heads. "Fall comes to the Garden of the Heads," he said, knowing that Rustum would be behind him, for he had seen Rustum hurrying across the street as he entered the gate.

"Fall?" Rustum looked perplexed and took a book from a pocket.

"Good morning, Rustum. Yes, fall. Autumn, the sear, the yellow leaf, the golden grove unleaving, the harbinger of winter, the death of summer, the coming of maturity and old age, wisdom, and ripeness. If wisdom can exist in a world such as ours." Frank sat on a bench, patted the place beside him. "The garden is beautiful today, but don't let that fool you."

"Good morning." Rustum sat beside Frank, leafed through his book and smiled. "Fall, yes. Cold come soon. Wind."

"No doubt. I understand the Caspian snatches all the winds from Asia and funnels them into Baku. The name of this city means windy place in some ancient language. Or is it burning place?"

"Asia." Rustum pointed toward the sea. "That way."

"Rustum. You have the name of a famous Persian warrior who killed Sohrab, his own son, in battle. Yet he loved the boy. The poison in the mixture was pride. Your new friend, Sambah, is proud. I've seen it in the curl of his lip when he listens to my monologues, though he pretends he doesn't understand English. Here, Rustum. Give this to your friend Mohammed Sambah." He handed Rustum an envelope.

Rustum frowned at the envelope. "Yes. I understand. A gift for Sambah, yes?"

"Yes. Look. The seed woman cometh." Frank gestured toward a woman coming into the garden.

"Cometh?" Rustum opened his book.

"Venus of Willendorf with a head. Look at her, Rustum. She's beautiful, if you see her as the ancients did."

Rustum took a pad of paper and a pen from a pocket. "Venus," he said, writing on the pad. "Vil-en-dorp. So many English words."

"How old do you suppose she is? Sixty? She looks like a Russian peasant. Where do you suppose she gets the seeds she sells?"

"Woman not from sea. She from war in Karabakh. You want seeds?" Rustum stood, dug in a pocket.

"From a war, Rustum? But she seems happy, she hums. Does a woman who comes from a war sing in happiness?"

Vafa cut her eyes toward the foreigner and the clerk, saw Rustum begin the ritual of searching his pockets for manat. They would, she knew, both buy some of her sunflower seeds. She sat on the bench opposite theirs, put her sack of seeds between her feet, and took a magazine from the seed sack for making paper cones.

Rustum pulled money from his pocket and came toward her. He will ask me my name, she thought, as always. He will ask in Russian, then switch to Azeri when I do not understand. She filled a cone with seeds.

"Woman from Karabakh," Rustum said in Azeri, "good morning. I am sorry that I do not remember your name. I am Rustum."

"I am—" Vafa hesitated. She disliked saying her name, hated the memories that came with hearing herself speak the sound. "Vafa," she whispered.

"Yes, Vafa, Vafa." Rustum closed his eyes as he spoke.

She knew he was trying to learn her name, but the repetition brought back the memory of her father saying, "Listen, the Armenian shelling sounds like someone calling your name: *voff, voff, voff*—like a child calling for his auntie Vafa in the night." It was a joke, and he laughed even with sadness in his brow. He told his joke two days before the shells fell on his house. A goat and a chicken walked out of the dust and stones, but her father did not. A week after, as she carried water from the well, she heard the sound of her name in the soft voff-voff-voff of the firing, then watched her own home fall into a heap of rubble, and her son, her son . . .

Vafa shook her head and forced a smile as she offered the cone of seeds to Rustum.

"Are you happy selling seeds on such a beautiful day?" Rustum took out a pocket knife and stepped to a rose bush beside the brass head of the poet. He cut a yellow rose, took it to Vafa.

"Happy?" The question astonished her. "Happy." She raised her brows and smiled at the stupidity of the question. "I cannot take the rose.

The guard for the department of refugees will think I stole it and send me from the garden."

She had seen the guard a week before when she went into the building at the end of the courtyard. Demetre. He looked Russian—tall, broad-shouldered, hair like a crow and a moustache that glistened. He would not allow her to enter after she said she was from Karabakh. "This is the United Nations High Commission on Refugees," he told her in perfect Azeri, speaking as if to a child. "You are not a refugee. You are an internally-displaced person."

She wanted to tell him about the shelling that spoke her name, about the stones crushing her father, about her home falling on her son. She wanted to tell him that her husband had vanished into the fighting with the Armenians. She wanted to tell him that she felt much like a refugee when she fled the Karabakh and walked for days to reach Baku. Instead, she smiled, gave him a cone of seeds, and said, "May you know the blessings of God."

Frank watched Rustum fumble with the rose, embarrassed to be rebuked. Like a lover paying court, he thought, and being rejected by the Venus of Willendorf, turned back with only a handful of seeds from the goddess, so he returns clutching the yellow flower of denial like a wound. Frank chuckled.

As Rustum sat again on the bench, placing the flower beside him, Frank heard the rattle of the iron gate. "Look, Rustum. Here comes Sambah."

"Yes. Friend." Rustum stood to greet Sambah. Frank gestured, inviting Sambah to sit with them.

The gate again rattled. "The secretaries for the High Commission," Frank said. "Look at them—young, ample, lovely. Imagine the Venus of Willendorf before she bore twelve children, before she ate fish and butter for sixty years, before she spread into the magnificence of godhood. Imagine that, and you have the young women of Azerbaijan." He waved to the secretaries as they paused to buy seeds from the old woman. They giggled, waved at him.

"Ample," Rustum said, taking the book from a pocket. "What is zis *ample*?"

"Ample, indeed." Frank stretched his legs and put his arm on the length of the back of the park bench. Sambah leaned forward as if afraid he might be touched. "Any one of those girls could conceive, carry to term, then squat and give birth without ever uttering a sound. Look at those magnificent hips. Each young Azeri woman looks like the earth mother herself. The women are descendants of the goddess, their bodies made in her image, and they have lived around the edge of the Caspian Sea for a hundred thousand years. Eyes huge and dark. Lips full enough to break your heart. Cheeks that want kissing. Bodies rounded into Renaissance womanhood and breasts enough to suckle an entire generation."

"Conceive." Rustum frowned and wrote the word onto his pad. "Kissing. Breasts." He shook his head, made clucking noises with his tongue. "So much English to learn."

"They walk through this garden every day, past the brass head of the Azeri woman who was a poet, past the statue of Stalin's friend Narimanov. Past the other brass statues. And the young goddesses never look at them. Maybe they are unaware of the bullet holes in the faces of the brass heads. Maybe they don't know about the rampage of the Red Army back in 91. They see the flowers, the fig tree, the pines, the beauty in the Garden of the Heads. They don't see the poison."

"Poison." Rustum flipped through his book.

"Yes. The fountain. It is a gift of mother earth, this water. You drink from it. The women from that building take water inside for tea. The water looks clean, but has its own poisons. It needs boiling, and even then there are the heavy metals from industrial pollution. The fountain is both a gift and poison. And there, look, among the roses, see the dumb cane? It will die in the winter, so why the High Commission staff plants it here is a mystery to me. For its beauty, I suppose. But if you were ever hungry enough to nibble upon that cane, the alkaloids in the sap would make your tongue swell so large you couldn't utter a word. That's why it's called dumb cane. And up there, on the wall at the end of the garden. Guards for the country's president carry automatic rifles. They look like boys at play, but they carry weaponry that can do more than drill holes in the faces of brass statues. This is Rappaccini's garden, lovely and poisonous and inhabited by an ancient goddess with her bag of seeds. Young females yet to be deified stroll through, jiggling and beautiful beyond expression. Their beauty is a gift, and it will be their undoing. It will invite attention from young men, invite children and hands red from laundry, backs stiff from carrying water, invite the hastening of their demise into the splendor of godhood."

Rustum frowned, wrote down some words.

Sambah edged farther down the bench. "You say such strange things."

"So, Mohammed Sambah, you speak English. But I knew that. Demetre said you are without work, that you came from Sierra Leone to

24

escape death in your country's civil war, that the High Commission claims you fled for economic reasons, so they will not help you here. I would help, if I could, but I don't know the trick of it." Frank stood. "Please. Keep your seats."

"Trick?" Rustum looked in his book.

On his way out, Frank paused in front of the seed woman, leaned close to look into her eyes. "But you are younger than I. Amazing." He held up five fingers. "Five cones of seeds for the pigeons. Pour them here." He held open the pocket of his coat for the woman to fill with seeds.

Rustum took the envelope from a pocket as Frank exited through the iron gate.

Sambah scowled. "That man, Frank, is an English pig."

Rustum considered the words. "No. He is American."

"An American goat, then. He speaks in crude, terrible ways."

"Crude?" Rustum opened his book, found the word, frowned. "He is my friend. He teaches me English."

"No. He speaks rubbish, and he is friend to no one. If only you could understand the insults he has uttered about Azeri women. They are women of Islam and should not be treated with such frivolity."

"Insults?"

"Yes. I hate him for being so much the English pig."

"American."

"Yes, yes. American goat."

"Frank gave this for you." Rustum handed the envelope to Sambah. "I told Frank. You have job not yet. You eat nothing yesterday. Perhaps he gives money for food?"

Sambah ripped the envelope, peered inside, his face set in anger then turning to surprise. "Why would the foreign pig give me money?"

"Friend Sambah, in Baku, you foreign. Like Frank."

"Yes." Sambah took the bills from the envelope, stuffed them into a pocket. He blinked hard, rubbed his eyes, and said, "I hate money."

Rustum heard anguish in Sambah's voice.

25

Blood Money

"*Un conejo!*" Conchita grabbed the steering wheel. The car swerved in a screech of rubber, and Rolf fought for control.

The rabbit tried to jump out of the way, but it went the wrong direction. Conchita winced at the sound of the rabbit's body hitting the grill.

Rolf brought the car to a stop on the shoulder, beside the savannah grass. "Taking the wheel like that was not such a good idea. The car could roll. We could be killed." He kept his voice soft but aloof and frosty.

"I wanted to save the rabbit. But you killed it." Conchita sounded on the verge of hysteria.

"Yes, you killed it. Come." He got out of the car.

They looked for a moment at the body, broken and stuck in the car's grill. Rolf pulled at the rabbit. An ear came off in his hand.

Conchita turned her back and shuddered. "Do not. Do not."

"I have to get it off the car."

"But you do not have to pull the poor little beast into pieces."

Rolf tossed the ear into the savannah. When he grasped the rest of the rabbit, he felt the warmth and moisture of it. He threw the body into the tall grass, then knelt to wipe rabbit blood from his hand. Savannah grass could cut, Rolf knew, so he took care to rub only from the stem toward the tips of the grass.

When he got back behind the wheel, Rolf frowned at his hand. "It feels sticky."

"What you have on your hands is guilt for killing the innocent rabbit."

"The rabbit committed suicide."

"Do not be a clown. You killed the rabbit with your car."

"What does your mother say about guilt?" Rolf drove toward the distant mountains. Something seemed wrong with the car, but he was too concerned with addressing Conchita to give the car much attention.

"She says to be rid of it." Conchita rubbed her eyes. "She says guilt destroys, and she is right."

"Your mother is only partly right, Conchita. We must not feel guilt for accidents. My grandmother always said that we must cling to guilt for the wrong we do. It is guilt that civilizes us, that keeps us human, she said."

Conchita looked at her watch. "Perhaps. Can you go faster, Rolf?"

"The engine. Listen." He slipped the car into neutral and pressed the gas pedal. "It knocks."

Conchita scowled. "I hear nothing."

"It knocks." Rolf drove into the savannah grass beside the road. He pulled the hood latch.

"It was the rabbit. It knocked something loose on the bumper. The sound is nothing. Nothing. We must go on or we will be late."

"I hate it when you whine like that. But at least you no longer weep about the dead rabbit." He got out of the car. She looked at her watch.

When he lifted the hood, the knock became louder. He touched the radiator cap. Not too hot. What else to check? he wondered. The oil. But should I check it with the car running? Perhaps not. And there's no way he would kill the engine out in the middle of nowhere. El Tigre was 30 kilometers back, though he did remember passing a service station. Ahead is nothing, he thought; the resort is over a hundred kilometers up in the foothills. A running engine will get you somewhere, perhaps. A dead engine might not start.

Then he remembered the distributor. Maybe that's it. He frowned, trying to remember the function of the distributor. Once he watched Pablo pop apart a distributor and reconnect some loose wires. I could do that, he decided: I could open it to see if everything inside looked connected. He called out as he walked to the back of the car: "Conchita, open the glove box and push the button that opens the trunk."

"No."

At first her response did not register with him. Then he heard, and he stepped to the passenger side of the car. "No? Why not? I need a tool from the trunk."

Conchita struck the dash with a fist. "This car is a goat. But it runs, and who cares if it knocks or does not knock? It will take us to the resort. Get in and drive."

Rolf closed the hood. He kept his eyes locked on Conchita's as he walked around the car. She set her jaw and lowered her eyelids. Like a peevish child, he thought. The spot on his cheek that he had named *El Ladrón*—the thief —gave a flicker of motion. When he touched the place below his right eye, the movement stopped. He got in and made a U turn.

Conchita slammed the dashboard again. "No, No, No. Do not go back home."

"Conchita, Conchita." He spoke as to a child. "We will ruin the engine. It's not worth it. We might be stranded on the road."

"Goat! You are the goat, not the car. It was that stupid rabbit." She sat back and chewed on her knuckles. After some minutes, she said, "You will stop so I can make a call of nature. Find a good facility, for I cannot stand to go on the ground."

It was news to him that she had such scruples about relieving herself. He had seen her squat behind bushes too skimpy to hide a mouse. Rolf stopped at a filling station on the edge of a village. She went first to the pay phone, then to the facility.

Back in the car, he said, "Who did you call?"

"Does it matter?" She turned her face to the window.

As they entered El Tigre, she said: "Do not expect favors tonight."

The spot on Rolf's cheek twitched. *El Ladrón.* It robbed him of dignity, the way it jumped around, and it robbed him of energy. It didn't make any sense that a nervous tic should drain him of the will to move about, but when it got started, it would do just that. Sometimes it would twitch for days non-stop, day and night. He rubbed it, trying to force out the tension before the tic began in earnest.

But it was too late. The old familiar flutter told him that within an hour, *El Ladrón* would be hard at work, moving his cheek about, robbing him, robbing. He glanced at her. "Shall I take you to your sister's place or your mother's?"

A look of alarm came over her face. "You cannot do that. Neither expects me since they know I'm your woman. It is almost a year that they do not expect me. So you will break up with me because you killed a rabbit and you think you hear your goat of a car knocking on something? What of my clothes?"

"Send one of your many cousins over for them."

"I'll come, for I have a key."

"Only to the doorknob. You will find the deadbolts shot into place to lock you out."

"Is this how you throw aside your women? On a sudden whim, and for no reason?"

"You are nobody's woman. And this is no whim. You have made it plain for months that you hold me between anger and contempt."

"Will you go to the mine tomorrow afternoon?"

"The mine?" Rolf stared, then shrugged. "To your mother's, then." He turned on a side street.

"No. To my sister's, you old goat."

"So it comes to that. I am too old for you. Conchita, the truth is, you are not enough woman for this old goat." He stopped beside a white-washed house with a corrugated zinc roof. "Tomorrow you may send your cousin for the clothes."

"Your manhood, it is small. Your heart, it is smaller even than your pathetic manhood. You never could satisfy me, did you know? Never. I hope you fall into the deep tourmaline shaft when you go to the mine tomorrow."

"When you become angry, you look like a piranha. White skin, fish-belly white. Teeth that protrude in a grin that is not a grin. Sometimes you are beautiful, Conchita. But not when you are white hot with anger. Then, ah then you are the piranha."

She got out of the car, slammed the door, and leaned into the window. "So will you go?"

"Go?"

"To the mine tomorrow."

"Why do you want to know?" He said it to annoy her, to stoke her anger. She stepped back, seeming shaken by the question. The response surprised him.

"No reason. No reason." Anger seemed gone from her, and she looked to Rolf like a child. An abandoned child.

"I never have understood you." The tic in his face began its rhythmic pulse. He pressed *El Ladrón*, feeling the flutter on his palm, then dropped the car into gear and drove into the night, leaving her standing beside her sister's house. Guilt, he told himself, is not a good enough reason to take her back into my home. Guilt might civilize, but it can also injure. He sighed. Living with Conchita for the last few months was like living in the eye of a hurricane. The tic below his right eye came often and stayed long.

The next morning, Rosa came with coffee. "Kona blend," she said.

He closed the door behind her, shot the bolt into place. "You know so soon that I now lock Conchita out of my home?"

"So soon. Yes. Señor Rolf, you are better without Conchita." Rosa set the tray of coffee in front of him and sank into a leather chair. "I can cook."

What was this? He raised a brow and looked at her, then picked up a cup. "You warmed the cups?"

Rosa smiled. "You like hot coffee, burning hot because you are much man. I noticed, so I warmed the cups."

"You are a gem, Rosa." He poured two cups, handed one to her.

"Conchita cannot cook."

"Everyone knows that. I am loyal."

"She was not?"

"She has many cousins who are not cousins. Many. I have a large nose."

"You are an attractive woman."

"No. Conchita is beautiful. I am plain. My teeth are crooked. I am a giant. My hands are big, my feet even bigger. You would go broke on shoes alone. Conchita and I have only one trait in common. We are poor women with enough Indian blood to darken our skins."

"And I am a rich foreigner with the light skin of the European. Does that attract you?"

"It does not repel me."

"The wealth or the light skin?"

"Both."

"I am old. Old enough to be your father."

"You are wise and kind. I have long seen that. Conchita is a fool."

"You would live with me?"

"Would you have me?"

"You are an attractive woman."

"No. But I am a loyal woman. Besides, Conchita does not want children."

"And you think that I do?"

Rosa shrugged.

The next day Rolf stood at a window and watched as Conchita and her cousin approached his apartment. He drew the shade against the midday sun. "She comes for her clothes, even as she said on the phone. With her cousin. Rosa, remind her that only her cousin is to enter the house. Let him take all of Conchita's clothes out to her. She is not to pass through that door. I will retire to the guest room, now, for I have no desire to see her."

From the guest room, he could hear everything in the apartment. He listened to Conchita's surprise at seeing Rosa.

"You have already rearranged the furniture in the living room." Conchita's voice had a hard quality to it. "He has had his hand up your dress for many months, then. The goat."

"Step back out. My orders are clear: you are not to come in."

"The goat is not home, then?"

"El Señor is not available, no."

"*El señor*, you say—my my but aren't we the fancy foot lickers. The goat has gone to the mine, I suppose."

"Suppose what you will, Conchita. And who are you?"

"I am Rodrigo. Conchita's cousin."

"Yes, and I am Conchita's fairy godmother. But it matters not who you are. Go through that door to the first closet. You may empty it of all clothing. No, no, Conchita. You remain outside."

"And if I refuse?"

"Then I call my brother. He said you would give trouble, so he parked below. Look you, there, in the street. The police car. Yes. Wave to him Conchita, for he says you have good and active hands. My guess is that he should know. Most men around here know such things about you."

"Bitch! I have always known you to be a sneaky bitch, Rosa. For how long have you lifted a leg for my man, even while I lived in this apartment with him, taking him every night? We mated like rabbits, did you know? Every night, and often in the morning once, twice. And then he ran to you for more. He will be grunting and slobbering on you until you cry for help, until you wish you had never seen the European goat. You will soon be on a chain, like that chain on his wallet. So much money he carries, like a fool. It is to control his lovers, all that money. Someone will one day kill him for the money in that wallet, and you will not have a money daddy anymore. The cash will be gone, and you will have nothing. He is an idiot, more stupid than a rooster and more randy. You deserve him."

Rolf smiled. He could well imagine the whiteness of Conchita's face, the toothiness of her grimace. *El Ladrón* twitched, and he pressed a palm against it. Rosa had stopped *El Ladrón* with a bitter herb tea and with a hot compress made from purple leaves. He should have noticed Rosa sooner. He should have angered Conchita sooner.

But why her anger over a missed trip to the mountain resort? And at the service station, what was that phone call about?

"I have all the dresses and four boxes with shoes, Conchita. Is that all?"

"It is enough. We go, now, cousin Rodrigo. And you, you bitch! Rolf will spend most of his time in that accursed mine, even as he is at this moment, watching men dig crystals from the dirt. When he does bless you with his presence, he will spend all his time tugging on your dress and pushing you to the floor. You deserve him, bitch."

When he drew near the mine, Rolf slowed. It made sense to him to park beside an out-cropping of rock that hid the mine shack from the road. That way he could approach the mine on foot without being seen.

The workers would be gone, for it was Sunday—all except for Pablo, the foreman, who had taken to sleeping in the mine shack since separating from his woman. Pablo liked the mine, liked gathering the crystals of tourmaline, beryl and kunzite. Rolf knew how fortunate he was to have Pablo as foreman, for Pablo stole nothing, and he so loved the fine stones dug from the hillsides that he counted it a crime if anyone split a good specimen with a careless blow of a shovel.

Pablo came first as pistolero, as a personal guard for Rolf. He carried a pistol in his belt and an M14 slung over one shoulder, for death could come fast and easy in gold country. Twenty-five American dollars would rent the services of a killer. Gold brought down envy, and envy left death in its wake. Rolf learned long ago that it was safer to dig for crystals of aquamarine and rubelite and kunzite than to risk the envy of those who searched for gold. They thought him crazy for digging crystals; they believed he made little from stones.

Someone had parked a motorcycle in the shrubs just outside the gate. The driver might have parked there in order to walk into the area of the mine. Or, Rolf thought, he could have been hiding the cycle in order to sneak in.

The shack seemed deserted. Rolf crouched behind a chaparro tree, blinking into the afternoon sun, searching for signs of trouble. He felt it coming, had felt it since listening to Conchita rail at him on the phone that morning. The exact nature of the possible trouble eluded him, though he identified it with Conchita and her cousins, with Conchita and her anger.

With caution, he approached the shack. The door stood a tiny bit open. It was unlike Pablo to leave the door ajar, whether he was within or outside. "Pablo?" Rolf kept his voice low. "Pablo?"

He saw only darkness within. With an elbow, he nudged the door open and entered. Inside, his feet seemed to stick to the floor, coming up with a wet, grabbing sound. He pulled the door open behind him, flooding the room with light.

Two cups sat on the table. Both contained coffee. He touched one. Still warm. The coffee pot sat in the center of the table. Both chairs were over-turned.

Pablo lay on the floor beside his bunk, his legs tangled in the chair. One of his ears lay on the floor beside his arm. The arm itself turned at an impossible angle. An obscene stickiness covered the floor, and Rolf stood in it. His stomach convulsed, and he swallowed hard. *El Ladrón* twitched.

How had anyone gotten close enough to hack Pablo with a machete? Rolf wondered. That the killer used a machete seemed obvious from the cuts on Pablo's face and body. Pablo had sat in a chair when the killer entered. Rolf squatted in the blood to examine the corpse. Pablo had fallen backward, chair and all, while the attacker or attackers hacked away. He never had a chance to reach for his pistol.

The holster on his belt gaped empty; the killer had taken the pistol. The M14 would be under the bunk near the table, Rolf knew—unless the killer had taken it, too.

Pablo must have allowed entry to the killer. Rolf looked at the other chair, lying on its side. Apparently Pablo allowed entry to someone he knew. Maybe it was the killer, maybe not. The person had sat at the table with him to share coffee. They drank, Pablo and this person. Then the guest attacked Pablo with a machete.

That didn't make sense. Rolf frowned and looked around. Pablo would not have allowed anyone to enter carrying a machete. Perhaps there were two, the guest and the killer, who waited until Pablo felt safe with his guest. Then the murderer rushed in, machete swinging.

Rolf retrieved the M14 from a sticky puddle under the bed. He jerked the blanket from the bed, used it to wipe the rifle. It didn't seem to help much.

As he stood in the doorway, Rolf became aware that *El Ladrón* was working away at his cheek. Yet he did not feel depleted of energy. He felt energized, ready. The killers were nearby, perhaps among the pits of the mine. He walked toward the rim.

Pausing beside a chaparro tree, he picked two of the large leaves. Native women sometimes used the leaves to scour dirty pots, so perhaps, Rolf thought, they would get some of the sticky off his hands. He rubbed, feeling the abrasion of the leaves. But he could remove little blood.

He deactivated the M14's safety and again walked toward the mine.

The mine was an excavation half the size of a soccer field. It stair-stepped down in something of a circle from the outer perimeter. Where the workers had found more crystals, they dug deep pits, for they received bonuses based on crystals they found. Along one edge stood shrubs; the other sides of the excavation were barren. Rolf circled the mine, heading for the cover of the shrubs.

As he approached, he heard voices: one male, one female. He belly-crawled into the shrubs. The voices became louder and more distinct as he neared the edge of the mine. One was the haranguing of Conchita, a sound Rolf had grown all too familiar with in recent weeks. The male voice is the one he had heard in his apartment. Rodrigo, the "cousin" who came for Conchita's clothes.

"How was I to know the goat would not be here?" she demanded.

"You swore he would be. I should have known better. You swore you would lead him to me at the resort."

Rolf nuzzled between bushes and looked down at the couple some 15 meters away. He set the rifle to semi-automatic.

"He will come tomorrow. I know it."

"Are we to sleep with that corpse, then? No? Perhaps we would sleep on the ground, waiting for the chance that he will come? I will not do it."

"Take the crystals from the shack. Dig this one from the ground. Look, it is over a meter long. That much kunzite is worth much."

"I do not deal in rocks. I do not dig up rocks. You have cost me much time, Conchita, and I grow weary of you."

Rolf watched Conchita back away from the man. He held a machete in one hand and pointed a pistol at her with the other.

So let him kill her, Rolf thought: then I kill him. *El Ladrón* increased its pace on his cheek. Let him kill her? No. I will feel too much guilt, almost as bad as killing him. I'll wound him, then.

With the sights set on the man's right shoulder, Rolf squeezed the trigger.

The man fired the pistol a split second before the rifle bullet struck him. Conchita remained standing.

She looked toward the rim of the mine. "Rolf?" Her voice sounded thin and strained. "Rolf? He shot my ear. My ear, Rolf. Look. I bleed."

Aware of *El Ladrón* jumping around on his cheek, Rolf made his way into the excavation. Conchita stood rock still, one hand on her ear, staring at him.

"Your cousin," Rolf gestured at Rodrigo who breathed in shallow gasps. "Rosa said you have many cousins. Kissing cousins."

"You will kill me now. I feel it. I feel death coming."

"Perhaps. Perhaps not. I thought we traveled to the resort for a holiday, but you were leading me to certain death, and all for what? Money. Is it so important to you, Conchita, this money?" He rattled the chain attached to his wallet.

"Do not, señor Rolf. Do not kill me."

Rodrigo groaned. Rolf stood over him. "He killed Pablo, and you helped. Pablo. My friend. Your friend. He poured coffee for you, and you thanked him by giving him to Rodrigo and his machete. I want you to shoot him now, Conchita."

"What?"

"You heard me. Look, there, on the ground beside him. Pablo's pistol." Rolf pointed the rifle at her. "Pick it up. Now."

Conchita stumbled toward the pistol. "He is already dead."

"No. His wound is bloody but not fatal. He could live. But you will shoot him in the face."

"No."

"Then die with him. I will shoot you both."

"I'll pick up the pistol and shoot you."

"Not possible. If you pointed it at me, you would die. Pick it up, Conchita."

She stumbled, falling to her knees beside Rodrigo, her hand bloody from holding her ear.

"Conchita." Rodrigo's voice came low, labored."

"The pistol. Pick it up. Yes. Point it at Rodrigo's face."

"Conchita, no." Rodrigo held a hand toward her.

Conchita started to stand. Rolf fired into the ground beside Rodrigo. She dropped the pistol and fell to her knees.

"You are clumsy, Conchita. Do not stand up. Pick up the pistol again."

She began to sob. "You will kill me. You will kill me."

"No, Conchita. I will shoot you only if you do not do as I say. Pick it up. That's a good woman. Lean over closer to your cousin. Yes, yes. I want you to put the bullet between the eyes, Conchita, the eyes that would have watched me die had we made it to the resort. The eyes that watched Pablo die. Now. Pull the trigger."

"You made me kill the rabbit. And now you make me do this. I cannot." She cried, jerking her shoulders. But she kept the pistol aimed at Rodrigo's face.

"You can. Do you feel your wounded ear dripping on your shoulder? He would have killed you if I had not fired. His next bullet would have struck your head . . ."

The pistol barked and jumped in her hand. Rodrigo became still. Conchita dropped the pistol and stood, her hand over her mouth. She stumbled back several steps.

"Can you drive Rodrigo's motorcycle, Conchita?"

"Yes. Yes. I—I think."

"Good. You will take it back to El Tigre. You will go to the bus station. You will buy a ticket out. Go anywhere you wish, but do not come back. Conchita? Do you hear me?"

"I—I. Yes. The bus station. Bus."

"Come." Rolf took a handkerchief from his pocket. "Hold this over your ear." He took her arm and led her away from the mine. She stumbled along in a daze.

Beside the motorcycle, Rolf turned her toward him. "At the resort, you would have watched him kill me. For money. This money." He took his wallet from his pocket, unhooked the chain that attached it to his belt. "Take it."

"You will shoot me now. I know you will."

"I am not a killer, Conchita. It is you. You killed the rabbit, remember? Then you and Rodrigo killed Pablo. Your last murder was taking the life of Rodrigo. You, Conchita. You are a killer. And for what? Money. This blood money. Take it, for you have earned it."

"I can take it? You are setting me free?"

"No one can set you free, not from the terrible knowledge that you are a killer of men. You will weep and groan under the crushing weight of your guilt, while I will live on, a man free from guilt, for unlike you, I have killed no man or beast, not even that rabbit." He slung the rifle over his shoulder, took her hand, and put the wallet into it. "You wanted to kill for this. You did kill for it. So it is yours, my once lovely Conchita. You think it is much, but it is a tiny part of my wealth. A tiny part, Conchita. It isn't worth trading for a single life—not even Rodrigo's, and yet you killed for it, so it is yours. Now. Start the motorcycle."

She turned to the cycle. "You will shoot me as I drive away."

"No. I send you to a worse fate, for you must face yourself even as you spend your blood money. It is you who are the killer, Conchita. You will leave El Tigre, and you will ponder your guilt for the rest of your life. Come back to your hometown, if you wish, but be warned that to do so is to die. I will put your photograph into the hands of five different men. I will pay each a retaining fee. Their instructions will be to kill you on sight if you return, but not to go looking for you beyond El Tigre."

Conchita put the wallet into a saddlebag on the cycle. She got on and kicked the engine into life.

Rolf watched her disappear beyond a bend in the road, watched the dust rising above the trees as she sped away. He turned toward his mine, feeling *El Ladrón* jump about on his cheek worse than it had ever done before, and he felt the energy draining from him.

Changing Zela

The Malay beside me held his kris at ready, the curved blade glistening, wet with rainwater and catching glints of early morning light. Behind him a Chinese fellow gripped his musket and muttered his native word for riches, "Wang, wang, wang," like a mantra, and the others, mostly Arab, crowded forward with their swords and pistols, eager for a fight and for the wealth of the Maratta. My men would change forever the lives of those in the slaver's town, perhaps change their own lives beyond returning to what they are now, but they didn't know or care. "We go in now," the Chinaman said. "Yes, now, Captain Trelawny?"

"No. We wait for the signal."

"Rocket not fly," the Malay said. "Too wet. We go now." He started down the hill.

"Stop." My voice came out a harsh whisper and carried enough command to stop the fellow. The town below remained silent, locked in sleep, and I imagined those sleeping in the houses soothed by the plash of rain, rare on this side of the island, soothed by the purr of the surf and by a belief in the vigilance of their guards at the three entries in the dirt wall around the town. "We wait." I fingered the rocket DeRuyter had given me, feeling it through the oilcloth, and reached into the pouch on my belt for matches, rehearsing the motions necessary to send my answering signal: hunkering forward to provide the rocket some relief from rain, striking the match on the hilt of my sword, touching the powder and aiming the rocket. Men behind me grumbled, one complaining in Arabic about cactus spines, another calling him a woman, but they kept still, perhaps because of the command in my voice though more likely because they had bunched up too much on the goat trail and feared brushing against prickly pear cactus growing in an abundance that astonished me given the jungles on the other side of Madagascar. DeRuyter said this side of the island got rain only during the monsoon, and that a scant amount, like the drizzle falling upon us as we awaited the signal.

When DeRuyter's rocket cut the sky, sputtering and sparking its way over rooftops, my men surged forward with a clank of weaponry, and I again had to command them to wait, this time grabbing the Malay by his tunic and causing the Chinese fellow to run into him. "Accursed cactus thorn," an Arab voice said, and "wang, wang, wang," Chinaman mumbled, some men chuckled low, harsh, nervous, and one man proclaimed in Arabic that he planned to steal enough jewelry to negotiate a marriage. I sent the rocket skyward where it joined a second one flaming over the city from the third entry to the wall. DeRuyter's 40 men would be entering the city in minutes, as would the 35 men at the other gate, so I had to hurry.

"Now." I pushed the Malay aside and went down the hill with my men pressing behind, a smaller group than the other two but better, DeRuyter had insisted, more fierce and battle hardened, men who would face down the Devil himself.

The gate wasn't much, just a hole in the dirt wall, and not wide though it gave room enough for my men to flow through like water. The guard at the gate stood, astonished from sleep and rubbing his eyes, pulling at his pistol and stepping from beneath a palm frond shed, his eyes glimmering to remind me in their beadiness of my father's attack crow defending ripened plums, a fleeting thought to amaze me with its leaping across the years into such a moment of violence. I hit the guard with a fast cut of my sword and felt my stomach lurch even as it did when I struck the crow with a stick, felt bile in my throat, hated the sound of the blade striking human flesh. Did I kill him? I didn't wait to see, for the men behind me would take care of him, if need be, and certainly the morning changed his life. I had to push on, to lead the men on toward the huts of the slaves, had to get to them fast, DeRuyter had insisted, for the Maratta would rather kill their slaves than allow them to be freed.

Gunfire and shouts awakened the city, and men poured from houses into the misting rain and dim light of dawn, men who appeared from all sides, men who slowed our progress toward the huts in the clash of sword and knife, the boom of pistols orange-red to leave black clouds of smoke drifting between houses and to leave Maratta lying in puddles. None of them seemed to have firearms, so my men cut them down like dogs, pushed into houses, yelling, slashing, coming out carrying whatever they could grab.

When I turned for a moment, when I shouted, "Leave it, leave it. Come with me," a blade bit into my leg feeling more like a burn than a cut, drawing a grunt from deep in my chest even as my arm swung the sword into the side of a small man with a face like a girl—not a girl, and not a

40

man, I realized, shoving him aside, but a boy and one to whom I had dealt a terrible wound so he dropped the kris he used on my leg, leaned toward me with eyes wide in panic. It was the eyes that made me push him aside instead of swinging again the blade. Another boy stepped back at my approach, flipped the kris in his hand and offered me the handle just as I might have as a boy if a man approached me, bloody sword raised, and the boy muttered something, a surrender I thought, then understood his Arabic mumble: "Friend, friend," though of course he didn't mean it, couldn't mean it after I had sliced into his brother or cousin, so he spoke from fear. I took the kris, pushed it into the sash around my waist, and said, "Lie down. Pretend death. Fast," not at all sure he would understand my choppy Arabic. He frowned, looked at the men behind me rushing into and out of houses, men bespattered with red, yelling men drunk in the frenzy of killing and looting, and the boy fell hard, rolled against the wall. Have I no stomach for this, after all, no stomach to be the agent of such violent changes in the lives of others? I asked without allowing the luxury of an answer for it was necessary to press on, to rush toward the line of huts, the white line looking like monstrous bee hives, low of walls and bearing thatched roofs, the huts of the slaves who by now, judging from their cries, had come under attack, just as DeRuyter had warned.

"The women will dispatch them," he told me the night before our early morning attack. "Old women, hags, fearsome in their red mouths from chewing betel leaves with what teeth the years have left them, crones with banana knives who hack and stab, whose job it is to keep anyone from stealing the slaves of the Maratta. God how I hate slavers."

We stood on the deck of the Grab, DeRuyter's deceptive little ship, and looked across smooth waters at the Corvette, close enough to see the Frenchmen on deck doing whatever they needed to do to prepare for the attack on the slaver city. DeRuyter dressed in the garb of an affluent Arab, as did I, the two of us looking no doubt like dancers in a London play or Arab traders in the markets of Isle de France.

"The men will trust you more," he had told me months before when he handed me the flaring pants, the blousey shirt, and the abbah, brilliant in blues, red. "They'll follow you as captain better for the clothing, and even better after you learn some Arabic." The clothing came from his cabin, larger than the captain's for he was the owner and often sailed on the Grab.

"So I am captain." I shook my head. "Such a change from being a seaman tugging on ropes in the English navy, such a change at age seventeen to become captain of a pirate ship."

"Never say that." DeRuyter turned toward me, his jaw set, his eyes flashing. "Never. We are privateers. For the French." He looked cold, hard, not at all like my new friend, the happy and strange American who had found me humorous, entertaining. Then he relaxed and slapped me on the back, the face of my friend returning with amusement crinkling the corners of his eyes. "And why not captain, if you were man enough to jump ship, to beat up your British quartermaster, to thumb your nose at the entire English fleet?"

Then later, after we teamed up with the Corvette, after I learned the Arabic words DeRuyter said I needed, after we had blown more than one ship out of the water with the subtle nine-pounders that appeared as out of nowhere on the sides of the Grab, after we determined to attack the slavers with the help of the French on the Corvette, DeRuyter and I stood on the evening deck of his ship speaking of the coming raid. "My best men will be with your party," he said. "If they have a flaw it's their propensity to whip themselves into a blood frenzy and to try stealing everything they can carry and more than they can carry. Rais will take tamer men, though they also are barbarians. In my party will be the ones most adept at creating the diversion you will need to get to the slave huts. The bulk of them will be the Frenchmen, and they love wine and women more than fighting. The captain of the Corvette, of course, will stay on his ship, hoping for good wine among the booty and hoping for a slave girl to his tastes, for he is determined not to let battle of any kind alter his pursuit of pleasure."

"That's disgusting," I said.

DeRuyter had laughed without being amused. "Yes. Disgusting, quite."

The leg wound slowed me but not by much, and I forgot it when the street widened, the walls ended, and the white huts appeared with cries of people under attack within their walls. The door to the nearest one, suspended with hemp rope, proved no obstacle to a slam against my shoulder, flinging it inward to the sight of a man bound hand and foot, stretched out on his back and a dark figure humped over him, her arms busy with a banana knife and the slave wriggling as he could to dodge the slashing. Another figure, staked to the ground, kicked at the old woman with the knife, a girl with her face distorted in the shadows and bespeckled with blood. Kill a woman? I thought, the bile biting hard at my throat, kill a woman? The old one glanced at me and renewed her effort with the knife, the Arab tied on the ground groaning and the girl kicking at the attacker to no avail.

I struck the old woman with the back of my sword, catching the side of her head and flinging her aside. She rolled into a heap of cloth to lie still against the wall, much as the boy had done when I whispered to him to fall; a quick prod with my cutlass convinced me she was harmless, changed but not dead, so I cut the ropes from the Arab slave, an old man judging by his grey beard and lined face, he struggling to rise but too weak from wounds, struggling to move toward the girl. "Spare her," he said in Arabic, "spare Zela, for the sake of Allah." He eyed the Kris in my tunic as I knelt beside him.

"Peace, gray beard, peace." I grasped the kris, an act that brought a wail from the girl and a look of terror from the wounded man; he watched with wide eyes and a prayer moving his lips as I flipped the dagger, took his hand and pressed the handle into it. "Friends," I said. "Friends."

He slumped back in relief, and I turned to the girl who held her wrists out for me to slice ropes but keeping her eyes on the wounded man, going to him as soon as I freed her. "Father, Father." Her Arabic came soft, in worried puffs of breath and her hands fluttered over his chest, pulling his shirt as in search of wounds.

Behind me a shadow darkened the door. A glace assured me it wasn't a Maratta but Rais, leader of the second group of invaders. Behind him stood Aston looking frightened, and beyond them, from the streets, slave huts, and houses came the sounds of our men, their frenzied voices, the discharge of their pistols, the clang of swords. "The rain has stopped," Rais said. "Quick, bring the slaves." He turned to the door but stopped when the wounded Arab spoke:

"Friend, my friend." He reached for me, and I knelt beside him, across from the girl whose hands still pulled at his clothing. "I'm dying, listen to me, listen—"

"You will live, you will." Zela's eyes said she didn't believe her own words, eyes black in the shadowed hut and glistening with moisture.

"Sheik," the man whispered, his chest heaving, "Beni-Bedar K'urchish ..." his voice trailed off as a look of determined fierceness came to his eyes and he pulled a ring from his finger, grasped my hand, pushed the ring on one of my fingers, took the girl's hand, drew it to his lips, and joined our hands. Perhaps he smiled as he dropped his head back, the fierceness going out of his eyes, his hands becoming limp, the death rattle coming from his throat. The girl wailed.

Aston vanished, returned. "Trelawny, we must go. DeRuyter says. The Maratta. Hurry."

"Come," Rais said. "Come. Maratta rally."

I stood, becoming aware for the first time since entering the hut of the wound in my leg. "Take her, Rais." But the man was gone and only Aston remained. "Then you," I said. "Carry her if need be." I turned to the girl, who clung to her father. The pile of rags against the wall, the old woman, moaned, stirred, and I thought she has a name, she too has a name, and I am crazy to be thinking such thoughts now. I loathed the thought of her rising, banana knife in hand, the thought of having to deal the old woman another blow with my cutlass, and I wanted only to get out of that hut—to get out with the slave girl, Zela.

She resisted me in her clinging to the dead Arab, but I picked her up, finding her light as a lapdog, wrapped my abbah around her to keep her still, handed her to Aston, took my cutlass. "To the beach. I'll stay beside you. Others will want her, and I'll cut down anyone who tries to take her from you, DeRuyter's men or Maratta." I shoved him through the door.

Slaves, hands bound, moved toward the beach, pushed by DeRuyter's men and by those from the French ship. Many of my men carried loot: small chests, rolls of linen, jewelry, and some few carried slaves, small ones and likely women. We had to wade into the surf, light and almost without breakers on this side of the island, to get to the boats sent from the Grab and the Corvette. Musket fire from the cliffs above the town urged us on, ineffectual because of the distance yet unnerving for the plop and sputter of lead balls striking the water. I scrambled aboard a boat, pulled Aston and the Arab girl into it. Rais joined DeRuyter in another skiff, the two talking and waving arms, their faces aglow with sweat and excitement.

When we reached the Grab, Aston and I lifted the Arab girl, still wrapped in my abbah, to set her aboard, and Rais strode up to her with an air of importance, ordered seamen to keep her separate from the other slaves. He turned to me with a wink and laugh. "The daughter of a Sheik. You did well, my English captain. Few men marry so well."

"Marry?" I stared in astonishment. "Marry?"

Aston laughed. "Yes, you are married. And she knows. Look at her. She knows."

My bride, eyes frightened and hair a tangle around her face, lay bundled in my abbah against the main mast, her face bespeckled with her father's blood and her clothing an eyesore of rags. "We are married?" I asked in Arabic.

She nodded curt and sharp, blinked at tears, and struggled with the abbah binding her arms to her sides. "Stay back," she whispered. "Back."

I moved away, feeling numb, thinking only that I knew her name, Zela, and she didn't know mine—yet we were married. Rais and Aston laughed and I whirled around in fury, hand on my cutlass. Both became silent.

"Easy fellow, easy," DeRuyter said from behind me. "Relationships shift fast in this part of the world, and your condition has just undergone a profound change, given what Rais has told me."

I turned in bewilderment toward the young woman. She struggled to squirm away. "Free her," I told Aston. "Give her my cabin. I'll sleep below with the crew."

"For one so young," DeRuyter said, "you show remarkable wisdom. Your kindness will change her life almost as much as your freeing her from the Maratta. And you, my young friend, Edward Trelawny." He laughed. "You will never be the same."

Talking to Catrina

Six left, I thought, only six so another firefight with Charlie would leave none, would leave me like the others who fell, just another body to sink with flies and grubs into leafmold turf. I took out the photo of my one-time wife, a laminated picture or it would never survive the heat and the sweat, and as always her smile settled me down even while I was aware of the shadow of the strawberry on her neck, one she tried to cover with makeup but I found it, figured out who put it there and so filed divorce papers, joined up and went through basic training and crossed the Pacific and bunkered into a hill where, new to jungle war, we rained nighttime death on the boys of Ho Chi Min as they drove mouse deer to clear the path of mines. That was before rain fell over the jungle enough times to wash holes in my heart, before we got shot up so bad there were only six of us left to slog through the jungle.

The lieutenant told us to bed down in star formation, which were his words for circling with our heads together and feet out like a starburst so if any hostiles appeared from any direction we could sit up and open fire without hitting our own men. Allen spread his poncho on my right, Joey on my left. We slept in our clothes, boots and all, which was fortunate for Joey because of what happened in the night.

"The latrine is under that durian tree," the lieutenant said. "Bury what you leave and don't smoke tonight. Charlie has a nose like a bloodhound and will find us if we hang any spoor on the wind."

"Snakes can find us," Allen said, glancing about, "spoor or no spoor. Cobras. Maybe king cobras. Or worse, there's the two-step, a little green fellow with a foul temper."

"A two-step?" Joey laughed. "You're afraid of a critter called a two-step? That's a dance back in Texas, a country dance. Why would anyone name a snake after a dance?"

Allen set his helmet under his head like a pillow. "It's a green mamba, one of the most deadly snakes in the world. If one bites you, you can take

47

only two steps before you die. And here in this jungle that ain't no dance."

"What if," Joey said, "one bites you and you're too smart to take even one step? Then you never die because it takes the bite and the two steps to kill you. You become immortal. Immortality through snakebite."

"There's nothing funny about snakes," Allen said. "Any number of those needle-toothed worms can kill you as dead as any bullet."

I bedded down damp with fungus working away between my toes and all of us reeking like a locker room so it didn't matter if we shoveled dirt over our latrine or if we smoked since there was plenty of spoor leaking from each of us for the wind to catch if any came up, plenty to grab the bloodhound nose of Charlie and lead him right to our star formation on the jungle floor, not that we made much of a starburst with there being only six of us left after the firefight that morning.

Allen watched me take the laminated photograph from my billfold. "You stare at that woman every night," he said.

"Yeah." I held Catrina, who looked at me from behind the plastic lamination, and she was a knockout in her fake buckskins, her beads and her million kilowatt smile.

"And yet she did all your buddies, and you had to get rid of her. That's weird."

"Yeah. All my buddies and some of my relatives."

"You didn't tell me that." Allen propped himself up on an elbow and reached for the photograph. "Lemme see her."

"She told me love is love and it wasn't my business to judge how she loved or who." I handed him the picture. "It wasn't a buddy, though, that put the strawberry on her neck. It was Todd. My brother."

"No. She diddled your brother and her married to you? No way. Your own brother put a hickey on her neck—that must have been a real downer. She is gorgeous, though. Gorgeous." He passed the photo back to me. "How come you look at her every night?"

"I don't know. I just do it, and seeing her makes this effing war a little easier to take." I didn't tell Allen that I sometimes talked to her and I imagined how she would answer. In fact she had started talking to me without my having to imagine it or look at her picture.

I looked at Catrina's photograph again, not with anger but wishing she had been able to commit herself as I had committed to her. I might as well have been angry at the insects for making the jungle so loud at night. Or angry at the fungus growing between my toes or the clouds for dumping on us or the durian tree for befouling the air.

"I hate that stinking tree," Joey muttered.

"If you'd just eat a durian," Allen said, "you'd appreciate the smell."

"Only a savage could eat something that smells more like crap than crap." Joey's voice went up an octave, and he sounded like a pimple-faced and burger-uniformed kid you would expect to find at a fast food counter, which is just what he was except that he wore damp combat fatigues and rested on the floor of a jungle in our starburst formation, his piece beside him ready to deal death. "One sumbitching durian tree stinks up the whole jungle bad enough to make you want to puke, and dumb slugs like you come along to talk about eating the stinking fruit."

"Elephants like them," Allen said.

"That makes elephants crap-eaters, same as the looney people who like to live in the jungle."

"No, listen. Vietnamese think the ripe pulp of the durian fruit is an aphrodisiac. When they fall out of the tree, they're damn near ripe, and folk gather the big spiky bastards, hack them open, and eat them."

"Nasty," Joey said.

"No, listen. Like I said, elephants eat the fruit and a lot of time they swallow them whole, and the fruit goes through the elephant to get dropped out. The locals poke through fresh elephant dung for the durians because the elephant guts ripen the fruit to perfection. You eat an elephant-ripened durian and you can diddle away for hours. Days, maybe."

"What a country," Joey said. "Cobras. Two-steps. The whole stupid country ought to be on a leash."

"The fruit is sweet, sugar sweet. Eating a durian is like sitting over the honey bucket in the latrine and eating raspberries. They're good to eat even if they smell like fresh dung."

"Eat raspberries in the latrine? Allen, you're one sick mother." Joey snorted.

"There's wild elephants around here. I aim to find a pile of elephant droppings and fish out a durian for you, Joey, and if you got any sand in you, you'll eat the gut-cured durian. What do you say, Don?" Allen turned to me. "Think we ought to get Joey to eat an elephant dung durian? If he starts stalking the mouse deer and humping water buffalo, we'll know the locals ain't lying about durian being an aphrodisiac."

"You guys hold it down," the lieutenant said. "Knock off the gab and get some sleep."

We did it: we scrunched around on the ground to smooth out lumps, and we went to sleep like tired animals, or at least I did in spite of the buzzing of cicadas, the croaks and bleeps from jungle creatures, the boinging cry of a bird that Allen called a night jar, a big goofy-looking bird that made electronic boings loud enough to be heard over the insects and frogs, though none of them kept me from drifting off and dreaming about Catrina, which is what I was doing when Joey started screaming.

It was shaping up to be a holy dream, with Catrina wearing only dangly earrings, and the ecstasy of our touching blended us into one, into a union so profound only a dream could do justice to it because words never would. I knew even as I dreamed and knew it to be a dream that what we once had, Catrina and I, was mystic in its beauty, holy, divine, sacred; and I wept, I lying on the jungle floor in a starburst formation with five guys who smelled worse than the durian tree—I wept while watching and feeling the dream of blending with Catrina; I watched my past self that didn't weep, didn't think, didn't know anything but the moment, the ecstasy, and sure didn't know she used her body to stir others, plenty of others, my own brother, into heights I thought accessible only to us. It was from such a dream that Joey's screaming jerked me back into the nasty jungle.

I snatched up my piece when Joey opened fire even while he screamed, and the staccato light from his barrel showed me a tiger holding Joey's foot in its mouth to drag him from our starburst, the eyes of the tiger surprised by the light and noise, surprised enough for the tiger to drop the booted foot, and Joey kept firing. The lieutenant got a flashlight beam on the tiger as it vanished among the trees and Joey stopped firing. "A tiger, a tiger," Joey said in his high-pitched voice.

We were all on our feet except for Joey who lay prone, babbling in a shaking voice, "a tiger," seeming unaware of the lieutenant's flashlight right in his face so we could see drool starting to foam around his lips.

"Stand up," the lieutenant told him, and Allen grabbed Joey like he was a child and stood him on his feet.

Later we went back to sleep, five us, with the sixth, Allen, sitting up like a spike in the starburst to watch for the tiger or for Charlie in case he heard Joey's firing or for snakes because the first watch was Allen, who feared snakes more than he did Charlie. The lieutenant said he should have posted a watch but didn't believe Charlie would find us in the dark or sniff us out with his blood-hound nose on account of the stink from durian tree giving cover for our locker room smell, and he hadn't even thought that a tiger might want to make a snack of one of us. Who would think of a tiger, anyway? the lieutenant demanded of us and we all shrugged because none of us ever heard of a tiger trying to eat an American grunt, and Allen said he always figured if a dangerous animal came around it would be a two-step.

The next morning in the green light coming through high leaves Joey looked at his boot, at the tooth marks, looked at the ground where his body left a scraped place from being dragged by the tiger, and he laughed shrill and high with a crazy edge to the laughter, an edge that set my backbone to tingling and made Allen pound on Joey's back like he was choking.

I wanted to take Catrina's photo out and talk to her but I didn't because of the other guys standing around looking embarrassed for Joey, so I made a secret of telling her about the tiger, told the story in little puffs of breath and making almost no sound, aiming the tale of the tiger toward the pocket holding Catrina's photograph, and I told her about the dream of blending. But of course, I said, it was just a dream and she said no, it was no dream because it happened, it happened, and her voice brought tears, her voice soft and warm, a hum against my breast there beneath her photograph and audible only to me under sounds of the guys cursing and under Joey's shrill laughter. The sound of her made my eyes sting into salt. I turned away, turned to pretend a search of the durian tree as if looking for fruit, and I whispered to Catrina in fierce, plosive words that I was sorry, so sorry. Her response was a puzzled silence, for she didn't understand, and all I could do was say, "I'm sorry, so sorry."

Two Men—Three Shoes

I lounged barefooted in the front of the canoe with a beer in my hand and singing a Hinson song when the river tried to kill us. "If you've got a girl," I sang,

"that wants to leave you
Every time some other dog sniffs around
Then jump that backyard fence and find a new one
Before that woman takes you to the pound."

Luke chuckled, probably because he is a fine guitar picker and singer and so has a good enough ear to recognize how I can't carry a tune in a bucket.

"So that," Luke said, "is a song that cheered you up when your old lady dumped your sad ass so she could make it with that stupid truck driver?"

"There's more to the song." I started to explain when the river took a notion to divide around an island, and we scooted into the deeper channel. I put the beer down and grabbed my paddle just as the turn in the river showed us a death trap.

The current ran us straight toward a huge tree, one that would have made a fine bridge if we had been afoot on the bank and looking for a place to cross. But we were in Luke's canoe loaded for four days on the river, and that tree had no business acting like a bridge. We ran smack dab into the bank with a muddy thud, into the very spot where the root ball of the tree had given way to the week's heavy rain. The canoe swung hard against the prone tree and tilted over, drinking the river and puking us and all our gear into the water.

I watched my shoes bob and vanish in the rush of current while I found footing in chest-deep water. "Luke?" I looked around in a panic in time to see his head vanish, and I knew the river had him. A glance at the bank told me I could scramble ashore, and in a split second I saw what the river would make me do. I would run down the bank, find Luke's body in a tangle of trees. The guys I knew called a bunch of junk like that in the

53

river a *sieve*. I'd see his red hair flashing in the water like a stop light and his blue eyes looking muddy in death. It would take hours to rig a way to pull him out of the sieve, and then what? I would be in the wilds of Texas, a jillion miles into trees and poison ivy, fire ants and ticks, too far to hike to civilization. Not that I could leave Luke because coyotes would see him as a meal rather than the good friend he was. I would whip out my lockback knife and cut a stick to whack any coyote that took a notion to nibble on him. My eyes stung at the fast vision of the end of Luke.

Then he came sputtering out of the water, a wild and worried look in his eyes. "I can't lift the effing canoe," he said. "I got under it and pushed up, but the current, the current."

With a fast dipping of my face into the water to cover any tears that Luke might see, I started grabbing for camping gear. It floated all around me, and I worked fast, snatching, shoving it into the eddy between me and the bank, waterproof bags of clothing, our cooler full of beer, ice, food; a bag containing the tent. The paddles floated, threatening to dive with the current under the log of a tree to disappear like my shoes did, and I grabbed both paddles.

Luke clung to the canoe, now on its side and jammed hard against the fake bridge by a current that wanted to push us under the log and among other trees jumbled like Pickup Sticks across the channel. The dang river wanted to shove us into the sieve where Luke would be, dead as a hammer, if he hadn't come popping up, swearing and looking wild.

"Good thinking, corralling the gear like that." Luke looked upriver. "I could wade against the current there beside the bank, holding on to roots and vines, and drag our stuff to that grassy spot." He pointed to a place some thirty feet upriver. "You stay here, keeping our gear around you. I could get on the bank right here, and we can haul the canoe ashore, empty it, then reload the gear and go far enough back to catch the smaller part of the river that runs around all these fallen trees. It could take hours, but we can do it."

"Good plan," I said. "Beats the hell out of guarding a corpse with a stick to keep the coyotes from eating it."

As he made it to the shore, Luke eyed me with a puzzled look. "Shove the cooler to me," he said.

His plan worked, and before long we paddled around the river island, beyond the sieve of tumbled trees. As we put ashore on a rocky shoal, a place to dry our gear, I spotted one of my shoes farther down the bank. We pulled the canoe to higher ground with me hopping about, cursing the way the pebbles and rocks hurt my bare feet. Then I went after my shoe.

Luke hooted with laughter when I came hobbling back, a shoe on my left foot, my right one finding every rock on the shoal sharper than the others. I took a few steps, hopped around in a fit of cursing, took a few more steps.

"Want to set up camp now?" Luke asked. "It's early, but we could dry out, rest, have a few beers."

"Wrong order," I said. "We can have a few beers and rest while we dry our stuff. Did we lose much when we flipped?"

"A tarp. The camper shovel must have sunk like a rock. One skein of water washed away. But we got lots of beer, and we can drink ice melt in our cooler. We're in good shape for the rest of the trip. Except, of course, for your one bare foot. Having only one shoe ain't worth much."

"It beats a poke in the eye with a stick. I'll rig something for the other foot so I can get around."

It seemed likely that I could make a sandal from using fishing line to tie a flat piece of bark or a bunch of large leaves to my foot. Something. But there was nothing to be had. All the bark I could find was crumbly, and the leaves on every tree and bush around were tiny and brittle.

When I finally figured out that I could empty my fishing bag, step into it and walk around holding the bag's handle to keep the thing on my foot, Luke again laughed like a fool.

"I should have let the coyotes have at you," I said.

"Coyotes?"

The fishing bag was okay, but barely so. Rocks still stabbed through the thin cloth on the bottom. Then it occurred to me that I could wad up one of my tee shirts, put it under my foot in the fishing bag, and get along well enough.

Luke took pity on me, offered one of his shoes. "Too little," I said. "I wear a size twelve."

"My size exactly," Luke said. "I'll take a rest, shoot down a couple of beers, and you can wear my right shoe while you do whatever the hell you need to do around camp.

His shoe fit well enough, though it was almost as wide as it was long. Still, it beat hobbling around on the tee shirt inside my fishing bag.

Luke watched me cast for bass. He followed me down the bank, wearing his left shoe and the fishing bag. When I saw how comical he looked holding that strap and limping about, I wanted to laugh, maybe loud and in his face. Instead, I turned my back and made do with a few quiet chuckles.

I cast a couple of times, pulled in a bass too small to keep.

Luke watched. "You said there's more to it."

"More to fishing?"

"The song. You know, cheered you up when your old lady up and run off."

I released the tiny bass. "It was a lesson, that song."

"So sing it. I could use a lesson about now."

"You'll laugh. I can't sing worth a crap."

"I might laugh, but so what? Let's hear it." He waited around, watching me cast.

"You laugh and I'll put a bass hook in your ear so it'll take you the rest of the day and all your doctor skills to dig it out."

"An emergency room technician ain't exactly a doctor," Luke said.

"Whatever." I waved my hand. After I heard plenty of silence out of Luke, I shrugged and launched the song way too high, so I growled the first line down to a range I could handle, almost. "I'm her dog now," I sang,

"No longer left to spend the night alone
I'm her dog now
Because she gave this poor old dog a bone."

I cut my eyes toward Luke.

He didn't laugh. "Yeah?" was all he said, then shambled off in that comical gait forced on him by wearing my tee shirt and fishing bag as a shoe.

It rained some that night, but the tent held. Just when I thought the rain had lulled Luke to sleep, he said, "So it wasn't the song that helped you because that song is supposed to be funny, you know—country and western redneck humor. Right up your alley. But you didn't even crack a smile over it. It was the new girl you found. I got to tell you that I'm relieved you found someone so fast. Still, I wondered when you chose this river if you might be suicidal, given all the rain and the nasty things flood water can do to a canoe."

"Suicidal? Me?" I tried telling myself that the idea astounded me.

"Your new girl—she anyone I know?"

"For a while she was an anodyne," I said and waited for him to express surprise that I knew the word, which I did not until I looked it up just before leaving on our canoe trip. Luke knows all those kinds of medical words, and I wanted to impress him. The rain increased, slapping the tent like water on a shower curtain.

"I was right to worry about rain," he said.

A few days before, when I told him about the stretch of river I wanted us to run, he had objected, but not much. "Lotsa rain lately," he said. "Could mean trouble, unless of course it's trouble that you're looking for."

In the tent he said, "Much more rain tonight and the river can get to our tent. We're not very high off the river." He turned on a flashlight, and I watched him struggle into a slicker suit. "I'm going to pull the canoe to higher ground. If we lose it to high water, we're screwed."

"Need help?"

"From a guy gimped up by having only one shoe? Nope. Besides, it's a one-man job."

He tugged the canoe up close to the tent, but it turned out not to be necessary. The rain stopped while he was fussing around out there, and the next morning I thought the river looked lower, not higher.

Around noon, though, we had to put ashore to get out of a bad rainstorm.

It was no ordinary rain but more like someone was pouring the whole Gulf of Mexico on our heads. The canoe took on bilge at a scary rate just from water falling from the sky. We found a highway bridge for shelter, and when we got out of the rain, Luke pulled his cell phone from a pocket. It was dry enough under his slicker and absolutely safe from water because he kept it in a Ziploc bag. While he messed with the phone, I knocked around under the highway bridge looking for something I could use for a shoe.

And I hit the jackpot: I found a shoe. Maybe not a real shoe, but it was close enough. It was a single thong, one of those cheap jobs that you keep on by wrapping your toes around a plastic strap that's attached near the front. I always hated them because of the way they flap around on my feet. By some miracle it was a thong for the right foot. But there was a problem, in addition to its being about an inch short.

It was bright pink. But I put it on anyway, and I clinched my jaw in thinking how Luke was going to laugh at me for wearing a girly pink shoe.

He noticed immediately, and he snorted out a few semi-mean laughs. "If I had a camera, you wouldn't dare walk around in that prissy shoe. But then I have something better than a camera."

"You have a digital camera in your cell phone." I lifted my foot, put it behind me.

"You going to hop around for the rest of the trip every time I pull out my phone? Then I gotta tell you that it's only a phone. It won't text, won't show me email, won't take pictures."

I put my foot down.

"What I have better than a camera is my memory. I'll never forget your wearing that prissy shoe." He pretended to stifle a laugh.

I ignored his attempt at humor. "The center part," I said, "the part that I wrap my toes around, is loose."

That piece of the shoe pulled through with a popping sound like pulling out a sink plug, and the shoe became useless. When the rain stopped, I hopped back to the canoe, rummaged through one of my bags, and pulled out a roll of tape.

Luke nearly busted a gut laughing. "Duct tape," he said. "You brought duct tape on a canoe trip? How redneck is that?"

I put on my best East Texas drawl. "My daddy tole me a man could fix damn near anything with duct tape. Iffn you can't fix it with duct tape or bailing wire, then it ain't fixable, he tole me."

To prove my point, I had that pink thong wearable in a jiffy—and I covered up some of the pink with gray tape.

As we pushed the canoe back into the water, Luke said, "How did you learn that big word?"

Took him long enough, I thought. "*Anodyne* ain't no two-bit word. It's common enough to them with any smarts. I learned it when I was a kid. Junior high, maybe."

"Bull. You looked it up to impress me."

"Did it?"

"Nah. What impressed me was how you said you got no help from your new girl in getting over your old lady's leaving."

We paddled a mile or two in silence, watching the river ahead since we had learned the hard way it wasn't to be trusted. Finally I said, "She treated me like a dog."

"But she gave you a bone. Or so you sang. I took that to be a boner."

"Maybe. But the price was high, getting chained up."

"Tried to control you, did she?"

"Tried, hell. Tammy was an expert in the control department."

"Tammy," Luke said. "I know a Tammy."

"No you don't."

"I do. The one I know is a regular fishwife."

He did that on purpose, and he knew I knew it, even if I couldn't see his face because he sat in the back of the canoe, and I wasn't about to twist around to look him in the eye. He would see right off that I had no idea what *fishwife* meant.

Before dark the river flung us into another sieve of fallen trees. I grabbed some branches of one of the big ones to slow us so the canoe swung around against it, and Luke hopped into the water to steady us so we wouldn't flip again. For an eternity of a minute we held tight against the tree, this one lying longwise with the current instead of trying to be a bridge.

"Hang tight to those branches," Luke said, though the warning was hardly necessary. "No way we're going to get through those trees down river. We're screwed."

"There's a window though the branches on this tree," I said. "I think the canoe will barely fit through, and look, a shallow wash beside the main channel. It's free of trees. If we can make it through this tight little tunnel, we get another chance at life."

With my tugging on branches and Luke standing on the log, pushing the canoe around, we made it through, and Luke hopped back into the canoe in time for us to paddle out of the river's second death trap.

When evening came we set up camp on the highest river island we could find, a spot just across from a country house perched on a bluff. The work setting up camp on that rocky island proved for me much easier for having two shoes, even if one was a pink thong. Mainly pink, anyway, since the duct tape covered part of it. Luke put up the tent, I made a quick job with the battery-driven air pump getting our air mattresses ready for the night. Luke climbed to a higher spot on the island so he could use his cell phone again, and I collapsed in the tent, dead tired.

The rain hit again, hard and furious, but I was too sleepy to care. As I drifted off, a woman's voice, shrill and panicky sounding came to me, and at first I thought it was a dream.

Luke scrambled into the tent. "You hear that?" he demanded.

"Sounds like Tammy," I said. The voice droned on.

"Listen. Listen to what she's saying."

". . . drown," the Tammy voice was saying. "There is a flash flood warning. If you stay on that island you will die. Come across the river. My son will help you up the bluff." And she went on and on about a flash flood and how the island would be under ten feet of water.

"Damn," I said.

"You don't believe her?" Luke said.

"Maybe not."

"I just called my uncle, had him check on the web for the weather report in the area of this river. He did. He said there was a flash flood watch."

"A watch. Not the same as a warning. I say we go to sleep."

"A watch can turn into a warning in minutes." Luke's voice was calm, mostly. "Maybe it just did since I got the report from my uncle."

"She sounds like Tammy." I heard a whine in my own voice, a complaining and mean whine, a sound I didn't like.

". . . you will die . . ." the Tammy sound-alike went on.

"Life ain't much fun," I said, "with every danged woman around telling me every move I can make. My wife did that for years, then she up and run off. Then Tammy jumped my bones and got me to believing in women again. But that crap didn't last. I say to hell with them, all of them. I'd a lot rather drown like a dang rat than be bossed around by women."

"So you did come out here hoping to die."

"Could be." I rolled over on the sleeping bag.

"I say we throw a few things into the canoe and paddle across the river," Luke said.

"In the dark? That could be suicide with the river running so fast."

"Staying here could be suicide. But I guess that's what you want."

It was a statement I had to ponder, so I said nothing.

"You're not a dog," Luke said, "And no woman can make you into a dog. Who wrote that song, anyway?"

"A guy named A. William Hinson."

"Never heard of him."

"He's an Austin songwriter."

"Maybe I have heard of him. Yeah. Writes songs so sad they can make a rock cry, and he writes ones that make me laugh. Like that song you sang about being her dog now. It's funny, even if you make out like it's deep. It ain't deep, just funny. But what the hell are we doing jawing about some song when the river is about to kill us? Not just you. Us."

"You go. I'll get some sleep. You come back in the morning."

"I ain't leaving you here to die alone. You know what would happen if a flash flood hits with us in the tent? We wake up with the tent collapsed all over us, with us zipped up in a bag we can't get out of, and the water tumbling us thirty miles an hour into trees we couldn't fight our way through even if it weren't for the nylon bag of a tent. We would both be dead in minutes."

The idea of being washed away in a bag of a tent got my attention, and I sat up to consider it. "That kind of death wouldn't be like drifting off to sleep from being dog tired, would it?"

"No. We would both be hollering and thrashing around, trying to find a knife to cut the tent away. And it wouldn't be just you dying because you think some woman zapped you into being a dog. It would be me. I don't deserve to die because your old lady ran off and because you think Tammy tried to put a collar around your neck."

"So what happens if we try crossing in the dark and the river spins us around, out of control, maybe into another death trap?"

"Look, you want to take your chance with crossing in the dark or stay here while the river rises? That woman over there lives on the river. She watches it. She knows stuff we got no way of knowing. I say we go across. Now."

The high-pitched wail of a controlling woman seemed to bore into me as the Tammy voice across the river went on about high water and death. Luke's face in the lamplight had more worry on it than it did when we were deep in the death sieves the river dragged us into.

"So you're saying you would stay with me if I didn't get into that canoe?" I asked.

Luke nodded, or I think he did. His eyes, so blue in the daylight, looked mighty dark and sad in the lamplight.

"Okay, then, damn it," I said. "Let's give it a go."

Luke's face brightened with relief, and he handed me my slicker suit.

The Greatest Name in Baseball

Jeremy Ryan tossed the whiffle ball. Just as he started to swing the bat, he saw his mother steer the blue Buick into the driveway. He missed the ball. "Ryan misses," he announced. "Jose Guzman is throwing heat that anyone can miss. But this time it might be that Ryan was distracted by the blue cup of ice tossed by a fan onto the field." Jeremy bent to get the whiffle ball. He gestured toward the Buick with his middle finger. "Ryan points at the blue cup. He's saying something to the umpire. I believe he's complaining about the unfairness of the distraction."

Jeremy kept up the running commentary while his mother got out of the car. He knew she would spend about five minutes fussing at him over nothing before going into the house and putting Vivaldi on so loud it would run Dad out of the house. She would sing along with it. Loud. "Dee tweet dee dee dee da dee dee." She called it singing, anyway. He tossed the ball again.

"Jeremy Taylor Ryan, you hush that up." Sabrina stood beside the Buick, arms akimbo.

Jeremy let the ball hit the ground without swinging at it. "Ball two. The fans jeer. The loudest boos seem to be coming from the general area from which a fan threw the cup of ice. Will Ryan pull it out for the Rangers? It seems unlikely. The Cubs are up by one. Top of the fifth in the seventh game of the World Series. A runner on third, and Nolan Ryan at bat with one away. This is Harry Caray calling the action, live, for sports fans across America."

"You're obsessed with baseball, Jeremy. You hear me? Obsessed. You know I can't stand a member of my family to be obsessed with anything. It isn't healthy, not for a ten-year-old. Not for anybody. Hush up or I'll take that ball and bat and put it where I put those stupid cards." She took a bag of groceries from the car.

Jeremy picked up the ball and threw it into the air. "A curve ball. It breaks fast but not enough to catch the corner of the plate. Ball three. Ryan steps back, knocks the bat on his shoe, picks up dirt and rubs it on his hands. The count is three and one."

"That's a nasty habit, Jeremy, rubbing dirt on your hands like that. You'll get ringworm from the dirt, do you hear me? Ringworm. Jeremy, would you hush and listen to me? I'm cooking some spaghetti tonight. You know what that means for your stupid whiffle ball, don't you?"

Jeremy knew. He tossed the ball and swung, tipping it off to his left. "Ryan swings and fouls toward third base. The ball bounces into the stands. A woman grabs it and stuffs it into a bag of groceries. The count is three and two." As he retrieved the ball, he kept talking in his best radio voice. He glanced toward the house and saw Mom standing on the porch, one hand on the doorknob, glaring at him. Jeremy thought her eyes fixed on him like an owl he had seen on *Nature* watching a mouse it planned to have for dinner. Did she look at dad like that? Probably.

Jeremy remembered how Dad used to play catch with him in the backyard, used to talk baseball with him. "Ryan is the greatest name in baseball," Dad said once. "And that's your name and my name. Ryan." Dad even took him to Dallas once to watch Nolan Ryan pitch, and Dad had joked about the greatest name in baseball being a distant cousin of theirs, though Jeremy knew better. Used to be, back when Dad played catch, he would buy Jeremy baseball cards.

An image of his baseball cards came to him, cards he had collected and traded for and memorized, cards he treasured. The image was the disturbing memory of the cards sitting in the bottom of the Dumpster, awash in spaghetti sauce. Roaches nibbled at the edges of them, and someone had raked older garbage across the cards, along with some crawly things. Maggots, maybe. As soon as he thought the word *maggots*, Jeremy had slammed the lid to the Dumpster.

The day he found the ruined cards, Mom had turned down the volume of the stereo when Jeremy came in from school so she could tell him that she had thrown his baseball card collection into the trash. Jeremy didn't believe her, not until he checked in his room and found them gone. He headed out back for the Dumpster. On the way he stopped in the doorway to the kitchen to announce, "I'll get them back."

His mother said nothing. She stood with her arms crossed, looking over her nose at him, smug and righteous. He thought he saw a look of triumph on her face. Mom the camel, he thought—her lips, clamped and puckery, looked like they weighed two pounds. They struck Jeremy as twitchy, rubbery lips, ready to draw back and spit in his eye. He had seen a movie in which a camel had spat on a shepherd boy. The boy's offence?

Playing too near the mouth of the camel.

When he got to the Dumpster and saw the way his mother had ruined the cards, he understood the look of triumph. And she must have been watching, he decided, because *The Four Seasons* got loud again just as he closed the Dumpster lid, and he heard her singing along.

Back in the house, he tried not to look at Mom. "I did it for your own good," she told him, yelling above the music. "Because you were becoming obsessed with those stupid cards. Obsessed. And no kid of mine is going to become obsessed with anything. You hear me, Jeremy? Do you hear me?" He had pretended that he did not.

Jeremy's shoulders sagged at the memory of the ruined baseball cards. He tossed the ball again. "Ryan swings and fouls. That's foul number thirteen for his turn at bat. Ryan might not get many hits, but he knows how to foul. . ."

Taylor dreamed of George's Pub where he liked to go when Sabrina made the house black with sound. George drew cold beer in a mug carved from yellow ice while Taylor dropped quarters into the juke box. He slid into a booth, yellow mug in hand, and waited for the music of Buck Owens to wash over him.

But something was wrong. The music. It was a tangle of yellow slimy things that made no sense. George perched like a turkey buzzard on the bar, his beak snapping, biting chunks out of the head of a drunk who looked like Jeremy.

"If you don't stop, I'll tell dad," the drunkard who was Jeremy told the buzzard, "and he will run away from us both."

As Taylor watched, George flapped vulture wings and flew to Taylor's booth to eye him with eyes that looked like Sabrina's. It stood, wings akimbo, screeching, screeching.

"Taylor Joseph Ryan," the bird said.

Taylor bolted upright on the couch. The vision of George-buzzard vanished into a weird yellow mist of cacophonous noise. Sabrina stood not three feet away, hands on her hips, glaring. On television, a man in a cowboy hat sang about being on the back side of thirty and back on his own. The words bounced against the violins of "Summer" in a terrible way.

Taylor realized what Sabrina had done. She returned home and found him asleep with country music playing on the TV. Instead of turning off the TV, she had turned on Vivaldi, and it was the clash of baroque and country that made the noise of the yellow mist.

"That moron cowboy is ruining my music." Sabrina jerked a thumb toward the television. Taylor stared at the thumb. A claw. That's what it looked like. A bloody claw, maybe from a hyena. The hyena babbled something at Taylor. He drew his shoulders up to ease a pain in his neck, trying to recover from the vision of George as a vulture biting Jeremy.

Was she singing? Oh, yeah: that was it. Singing. Sabrina's rendition of Vivaldi—though how she got those sounds from "The Four Seasons" was beyond him. "Dee tweet dee dee dee da dee dee." She had said something else, though. What was it?

He raised his brows, held a palm up, and asked her to repeat what she had said. The yellow mist from the blurring of Vivaldi with the cowboy's song hammered at Taylor.

Sabrina added to the noise, Taylor realized. She's trying to drown me out. She doesn't want to hear me.

Her nastiness hit him like a physical blow, and Taylor felt something he seldom allowed himself to feel. Anger. Red, ropy with fibers.

He held it in a delicious way, close to his chest, knowing he could reduce it to a thread or release it to explode across the room. Sabrina had never seen the explosion of his anger. Taylor had always contained it, kept it small and pink and inside--but this time. This time.

He let the red fibers play across his chest, holding, holding. What was she saying? Her voice came to him through the noise of the yellow fog. What was she saying?

". . . can't stand it for a member of my family to be obsessed with anything, especially with something so stupid as . . ."

Taylor released the red. It laced through him, lifting him from the couch in a slow, measured way. He felt his eyes narrow to slits, felt the red lift him over Sabrina like a mountain lion standing over a fox sparrow. She fell silent.

The red fibers, moving him like a puppet, took him to the hall closet. He watched, almost amazed, as his hands took out the bowling bag, took out the ball. Back beside Sabrina, he looked at her in the yellow noise, the violins of Vivaldi and the guitars and drums from the TV; she stepped back in fast, sparrow-like jerks. His arm lifted the ball.

Taylor could feel the red move the arm higher, higher. Sabrina fluttered back again. Taylor almost laughed. "You will never have to be bothered by country music on TV again," he heard his voice say.

Sabrina fluttered, stumbling, her arms flapping. She fell. Taylor watched the red that controlled his arm lift the ball higher, then smash it into the screen of the television in an explosion of glass, cleansing glass that showered the room, washing out the yellow mist, leaving only violins playing Vivaldi, violins he had loved like fresh-shined copper before Sabrina ruined them with volume and repetition that hung the air with the black of tarnished copper. He could taste it, black and metallic, even as the red lifted him in a leap to the top of what remained of the television.

After a few satisfying jumps on top of the TV, then flinging it to the floor, face down, Taylor allowed the red to recede to pink threads. He gathered them enough for stepping across Sabrina to turn down the black copper of the violins so he could tell her she had won.

What did that mean—that she had won? Taylor wasn't sure, but the telling of it felt like victory, not defeat.

He walked to the door, holding only enough pink threads to allow him a song of victory, a mockery of "Summer" and of Sabrina:

"Dee tweet dee dee dee da dee dee

Da dee dee da dee dee."

On the front porch, he looked at Jeremy tossing a whiffle ball. The dream image of George the vulture flickered in front of him. He tried to push it aside. "Run away from us both, run away from us both," the voice of the drunkard said. Taylor winced.

Jeremy picked up the whiffle ball. "That's foul number twenty-five. Nolan Ryan might set a new ballpark record for fouls here at Wrigley Field."

When he had heard the scream of Vivaldi start up, he knew Dad would soon come out, get into the Buick, and drive off. Resentment fluttered around him like the yellow-black leaves, diseased in midsummer, drifting from the locust tree in his backyard, the backyard where he and Dad no longer played catch, the yard he walked through to the Dumpster to find maggots crawling through the spaghetti sauce on his baseball cards. He felt resentment of Mom's chipping away at baseball. Trashing his cards. Using Vivaldi to keep Dad away, to keep him from playing baseball or talking baseball. Resentment of Dad for abandoning him. He saw his anger as a storm of diseased locust leaves dancing about him to the beat of *The Four Seasons*. "I hate Vivaldi," he muttered. Hate him, hate him.

But at least, Jeremy told himself, he had a piece of baseball left, a game of solitaire with a whiffle ball. And I'm Harry Caray, the number one sportscaster in the world. "Jose Guzman delivers the pitch." Jeremy tossed the ball and hit it straight into the hedge near the sidewalk. "Ryan connects. You can hear the crack of the bat all over the stadium. The crowd goes wild. Ryan races for first."

Jeremy dropped the bat and ran to the hedge. He glanced back at his dad standing on the porch, watching. Watching me? This is something new. It felt good.

"Wayne Wilson tries to catch the ball, but it hits the center field fence and vanishes into the vines. This is Wrigley Field, ladies and gentlemen. Vines grow all over the outfield fence. This will be a ground rule double." The whiffle ball, he knew, had to be in there somewhere. He pushed into the hedge, saw the ball, and reached for it without seeing the nest of paper wasps until it was too late.

"Yikes." Jeremy leaped back. Wasps flew right into him, stinging through his tee shirt. "Yikes. Angry fans pour onto the field." He jerked back from the hedge. "The umpire didn't call a ground rule double, and Nolan Ryan runs past second." Jeremy whirled around, yelling with each sting. He ran toward his father, making his voice take on the urgency of a great sportscaster. "They blame Ryan. The fans blame Ryan for the miscall. They pile all over him. Yikes. Ryan has to roll on the ground to get the frenzied fans off him."

Jeremy threw himself to the ground and rolled to squash the wasps. "He slides into home plate, in the nick of time, and the Rangers take the lead."

Wasps kept diving in, but something was knocking them out of the air. Jeremy stopped rolling and saw his father slicing the air with a towel. No. A shirt, he realized with a start. Dad took off his shirt to knock the wasps off me. Me.

"Even the umpire is in on the act, swatting crazy fans away from Ryan like so many flies. Ladies and gentlemen, never in the history of baseball has there been anything like this." Jeremy stood up and turned around so his father could get at any wasps that might be crawling on him. In the middle of a swing, Taylor hopped back and yelled.

Wasps are going after Dad. "The bullpen," Jeremy pointed at the Buick.

Taylor picked up his son and ran toward the car. Jeremy clung to him, talking in his best radio voice. "The manager is on the field. He kicks away the mad fans and now has Nolan by the foot. He jerks him from the frenzied people and picks him up. He's running for the bullpen . . ."

Inside the car, Taylor squashed two wasps with the heel of his hand. "Jeremy, are you all right?"

"Those things hurt."

"Yeah. They got me, too. You all right?"

"Sure." Jeremy was aware that he was on the edge of tears. "Why

68

wouldn't I be all right? The Texas Rangers just took the lead in the world series." He heard himself laughing in a way that scared him. Taylor lifted Jeremy's shirt and looked at the swollen places.

Wasps bumped on the windshield, then drifted back toward the front hedge. Taylor rolled his window down. "It's hot in here. If the wasps come back. I'll roll it back up." He fumbled for his keys. "I'm getting you to a clinic to have those stings checked out. Then. Then."

"Then?" Jeremy prompted.

"Then how about going to the park to warm up a couple of pitchers. Major league stuff, with two Ryans on the team. We will be a winning combination for sure. You can be the color commentator."

"Play catch at the park? Cool." Jeremy rolled down his window. "Listen, Dad."

"To what?" Taylor struggled to get his shirt back on.

"Vivaldi with static. Mom cranked the CD until it blew the speakers."

"Yeah? It sounds like black noise but without the taste of copper." Taylor laughed and started the car.

As Dad pulled out of the driveway, Jeremy looked for the wasps around the hedge. But he didn't see any. While they drove off, he listened to the Vivaldi static becoming smaller and smaller behind them.

Abu Hassan the Wise

"Wait outside, please," the doctor told Anwar, and he bowed to the request, for the gravel that peppered his face had done what others might consider only slight damage. The man who had stepped on the mine lay dead beside the road, another lost an arm, and Anwar still lived, could walk, could carry the weapon thrust upon him by a Pashtun who retrieved the rifle from the dead man. It was the first weapon Anwar owned, and he took pride in it—pride tinged with shame, for the rifle came to him at the cost of a life, and the dark stain of the man's blood still clung to the rifle.

Anwar ducked out through the door of the tent called a hospital and squatted on the ground close to another man. Three others also waited for a doctor, though to Anwar they seemed incapable of rising if called. One likely was dead, judging from his heavy stillness and from the flies that walked on his face, into his nose, and another lay sprawled, laboring for breath. The man beside him seemed to be studying Anwar, who worked at not noticing since such open scrutiny was rude, and Anwar felt embarrassed for the man, for his lack of civilized manners, for the gray in his beard proclaiming him old enough to know proper manners, the lines on his face that should be signs of wisdom but apparently were not. Except for his poor manners, Anwar thought, he looks like my father. He fought the impulse to touch the dried blood on his face.

"Did the doctors send you out here to die?" the man asked.

"No."

"No?" The man laughed, though his eyes betrayed no amusement. "I recognize you. From my mother's village in Pakistan, yes? It's almost positive the same ancestor's blood flows in your veins and mine, and that ancestor lived only a few lifetimes back in time. You are not Pashtun, so you get no treatment, nor I, nor these others. Ramix there is already dead, and look, my old friend Othar will follow, for I could not save them, nor could I show them how to save themselves. We are fools, you know. I am a fool, I Abu Hassan the Wise, I am a fool."

71

Such words should shame the man, Anwar thought, but they do not. He rubbed the dark spot on his rifle.

"You won't remove the stain with such scraping. It will take kerosene, and even then there's no help for it, no help at all, for what you see is not mere blood, oh no. It's the essence, the soul of the dead man, the one who carried the rifle before you. He will with dust and grit cause the piece to jam. Perhaps not today or even next week, but such a day as when you find yourself lying among burrs and cactus spines with only pebbles to protect you from the bullets that splatter all around, foreign bullets fired by those men from up north, the agents of Satan, your lieutenant would have you believe, squirting devil bullets to peck the ground around you like a crow, and you spot the gunman's turban bobbing above a ridge, the man who fires at you, and it seems such a simple matter to move the rifle sight to the perfect place for the kill, the perfect place to stop the bullets, and you squeeze the trigger knowing in that moment you will live at least another hour or day though the price of it be a man's life, a man with a turban and not Satan at all, or you know it until the mechanism of the trigger snaps into place without making the rifle cough, for don't you see?

"The rifle will jam, locked into silence by grime and that red smear, the spirit of the dead man who owned the rifle last, and you can only shrug, say one last sura, and hope the rules of the jihad work the way they told us back in Pakistan so you will vanish from this world to awaken instantly in the seventh heaven to dwell in peace and love forever, even if your comrades, crouching behind other pebbles don't see you in heaven at all but instead see you in hell, see your head fly apart, see shards of pink bone from your skull spike the ground not unlike the devil bullets still pecking around you and them so they know they might be next but of course don't believe it, for death is always something that happens to someone else. To Ramix there. Look at him."

Abu Hassan, Anwar thought, says such odd things, and yet he seems a good enough fellow in spite of being a bit cracked. Anwar watched Abu Hassan wipe his cheek on a sleeve.

"This Ramix, this young friend," Abu Hassan said, "thought he would find the keys to heaven. But is he in heaven? Is this the way of the holy war—to stagger with leaking wounds to the hospital tent where they turn you out for being Paki and not Afghan, to be pushed away with the promise of treatment soon, when your name is called though of course your name will never be called just as no one came to the tent's door to announce it was time for a doctor to see Ramix, so your fate becomes his in falling over like that where flies creep into your mouth? Is this what you envisioned when you joined the holy war? Perhaps you believe he is in heaven, this dead Ramix, that he bypassed the judgment, the reading of his deeds in the Book of Life, slipped beyond the divine event and cosmic judging to fly into the arms of dancing girls who offer melons and yogurt laced with honey and sweet mulberries, who offer lips for kissing and the sweetness of divine passion, so he is there now and forever with senses come alive to the music of love forever. Or is he merely dead here on the desert where flies come even on cool autumn days to walk across his face, to dart into mouth and nostrils in a grotesque dance that flies cannot do in paradise?"

"You must not talk thus," Anwar growled. He shifted the rifle, balanced it on his knee, gripped the trigger and pointed death at Abu Hassan.

The man raised his brows, nodded. "Kill me then, if you have the stomach for it."

I should, Anwar thought, I should do it. But he also told himself that he could not, for it would be a sin. He rolled the word around on his tongue, silent in closed lips, as if tasting the term, and it seemed important to spit it out, the word, to get it away from his tongue, for it drew back to gag and convulse in his throat. "Sin," he whispered. "Sin."

"What?" Abu Hassan's face show perplexity, perhaps over not hearing, Anwar thought, perhaps over the word spat into the air without context. So Anwar raised his voice:

"Sin. Have you no sense of sin?" Anwar reached toward the sting on his face, caught himself and pretended he had raised the hand to scratch his neck.

"Ah. That one, sin. Yes." With smoothness of motion that astonished Anwar, Abu Hassan stood, reached into a pocket, and pulled out a skull-cap. He again squatted, removed his turban and set the cap upon his head. "I earned the right to this with my Haj, my pilgrimage to Mecca. Eight times around the Kaaba I went—you look surprised that I said eight and not seven—I went beads in hand, and in the daylight with all the other thousands, most in a trance of religious fervor, a huge African striding beside me, beyond me, his mouth moving and eyes bulging though they didn't see the small fellow he kicked aside, an Indonesian perhaps from the size of him, and I stopped to pick him up, which I should not have done, so I went around an extra time, yes. Eight times, for one didn't count when I stopped prayer and holy thought to pick up the little man. Then to the other rituals of Mecca. These hands."

73

Abu Hassan rubbed his hands together, looked at them. "These hands. With them I have dispatched the enemy in battle, seven of them with my own kind of devil bullets, Russian, hah, or Chinese bullets, seven to fall into dirt and heat and fleas. Is it a sin to kill thus? With these self-same hands I cast stones at the devil near Mount Arafat where the prophet once stood. That was it, the sense of sin, yes, that was it, and perhaps my eyes bulged unseeing like the African when he stepped on the small man, and perhaps my mouth moved like his did; perhaps I prayed while casting the stones—it's hard to remember because of the heat and the dry, and more than once that day I wished the Haj could occur during another month, that my Haj could come earlier or later when the sun didn't strike with such fury. Some fell from it, the sun. They fell and their tongues lolled out, and the Saudis had to haul them away or they would have died, stamped into the ground by the faithful in their swirl around the Kaaba, and maybe some did die. While brothers lay sick from the sun and in danger of dying, I went on with the ritual of the Haj, though not without a sense of sin and a sense of shame. Lunar months slip around the calendar, so if I waited the sun might be less brutal, but who thinks such thoughts in the face of the Kaaba or Mount Arafat or Mena?

"Yes. I have had a sense of sin, shame even for this war now and a more intense shame than I had for wishing the calendar different so I could be pampered during my Haj." Abu Hassan shrugged; Anwar thought the gesture had more to do with his eyebrows than his shoulders. "But that was in another country. And here? Is there not sin and shame in killing?"

Seeing the skullcap and hearing the mention of holy places made Anwar feel like he imagined a candle might feel while burning in a hot desert night: limp, almost fluid. His hands shifted the rifle, an act that seemed to have nothing to do with volition, Anwar noted as he watched the rifle stand on its butt, harmless to all around him, and he was glad that the madman who called himself Abu Hassan the Wise fell silent and looked elsewhere, eyes unfocused, for it gave Anwar the opportunity to explore with fingertips the wounds on his face. They felt rough, scabbed, and he noted that they moved beyond pain into a dull itch. Good, he told himself; an itch means healing. This man cannot be wise, Anwar thought, to say such outrageous things. He must be mad.

The madman coughed, leaned, caught himself and remained upright. Another who looked almost as far gone as Ramix drew up, rolled to one side with faint moaning. Abu Hassan touched the Haj cap, and his eyes seemed to focus as he turned toward Anwar.

"What? You haven't killed me yet? You will, though perhaps not today."

"You carry no weapon." Anwar waved a hand, indicating the others awaiting medical help. "Nor they. Are you not soldiers?"

Abu Hassan drew an arm against his ribs and winced. "They lost their rifles when they were wounded, for men without wounds had no weapons and took them. I discarded mine long before the shrapnel pierced my side."

When dusk came the doctors had not called Anwar's name, nor that of Abu Hassan or Ramix or any of the others turned out to wait. Anwar struggled to his feet, using the rifle to steady himself, and walked toward a mosque for his evening prayer, though no imam chanted, and the air carried only the sounds of distant trucks, of crows cawing out the dark sounds of death, of his own feet scraping pebbles on the road, of the stumbles of Abu Hassan, who seemed to be following him. He still watches me, Anwar thought, and resolved not to touch his own face, to make himself seem impervious to the gravel wounds.

Buildings lay in ruins from a bomb or from shelling or from an earthquake, though most homes still stood in the village. The spires of the mosque, squat in their poverty and dusted from decades of desert wind, lifted above other buildings to guide him toward evening prayer. Anwar figured the imam would be up there already, ready to chant the call to prayer when the correct moment arrived. He remembered an uncle who once traveled to India returned to tell of mosques that played recordings of the call to prayer, but Anwar didn't believe it. No Moslem, he affirmed, would dare reduce the call to prayer to a commercial recording— and if one ever did, true believers would rip the recording device from the mosque, smash it into the dirt. As he neared the spires, Anwar noticed the sounds of trucks became louder—trucks and perhaps a tank or two, old ones left over from the war with the Russians. And still, he thought, puzzled, the imam does not begin his chant.

When he turned a corner where the street opened to the mosque, Anwar understood: people feared going into the mosque. Pashtun soldiers parked their military trucks and tanks beside the mosque as a guard against bombs, an act that kept the villagers away from the building, for none believed such proximity would do more than bring destruction to equipment and mosque alike. "But what do I care?" he whispered in a throaty rumble that startled him with its tone of weariness and despair. Let others fear for their own life, he told himself, for I came seeking glory or death, and what greater glory than dying while saying prayer, except perhaps for victory in the jihad? I'll pray in the mosque, though I be alone.

The thought of his own bravery gave Anwar a tingle along his spine, one that he also identified as fear. He walked between two tanks, dusty, smelling of grease and gasoline, and stopped beside the entry to the mosque to remove his shoes. The whole world is a mosque, he told himself, and the true believer can say prayers anywhere. Anywhere. He pulled at a shoe lace, causing it to break, and he mumbled the beginning of a curse before catching himself, changing the curse into a lament for his shoes. So old, he told himself, and patched and leaking air through to socks that also had holes and patches, not socks or shoes fit for a soldier and especially not fit for a campaign in winter that could take him into the high snows. He had watched with disgust as Pashtun fighters pulled boots from dead comrades after Alliance soldiers dropped shells among them. Like chickens, he thought, scrambling to get the best scraps, or worse like dogs, those unclean animals, snarling and snapping in their greed.

After tying the broken shoe lace back together, he glanced up, seeing Abu Hassan staring at him through the gap between Russian tanks. The man nodded, pursed his lips as in understanding, and Anwar looked at his hands, which had automatically began tying the laces as if he no longer intended to remove the shoes for entering the mosque.

"Come with me, brother." Abu Hassan offered a hand. "We'll make a mosque of the field beyond the doomed building. Your decision not to go inside shows such wisdom that I shall make a gift to you of my old name, for I am a fool now, and you should be called The Wise."

It took a moment of staring at Abu Hassan's hand for Anwar to realize the man was right in knowing Anwar had decided not enter the mosque. He grasped the hand, pulled himself to his feet, took his rifle, and followed Abu Hassan.

"Ramix died," Abu Hassan said.

"Yes." Anwar remembered the flies.

"And Othar. Without medical help others will go soon, and they will get none from the Pashtun doctors, who are busy saving their own tribesmen. Are the doctors not Muslims? Are we not all of Islam?"

Soldiers who parked the trucks and tanks had fled, or so Anwar assumed, though he considered it possible some of them watched from the shutters of nearby houses. "What of your wounds, Abu Hassan?"

The man stopped, turned in astonishment. "You know my name? But no matter. I spoke it, right? In my chatter, so of course you know." He resumed walking. "Only one of the wounds afflicts my body. The other wounds are less easy to perceive though they grieve me more than the hole in my side, that slow leak that lets slip my soul, drop by drop becoming a smear like that on your rifle. Sudden death would be better, for perhaps then if only for an instant could I believe martyrdom was upon me and I entering heaven. Or I might have believed that weeks ago."

"You speak blasphemy."

"I speak my truth, and you must take it as you will." Abu Hassan glanced at the sky. "They will come, I can feel it. Tonight. There, look, across that field, some rocks flat enough to be clean, and a gully beyond. I carry no prayer rug, nor you, so the rocks will serve, and I know the direction of the Kaaba in Mecca."

He pointed with a wave of his hand, and Anwar thought him right in choosing west to southwest. He glanced back at the mosque looming in the dark above the stains that were tanks and trucks, and still, he thought, no imam, no chanting to the faithful, and no worshipers daring to venture where a bomb might streak down. So I pray with Abu Hassan the Wise who has given me his title and now considers himself a fool, pray with one who has been to Mecca, perhaps has drunk from the spring at Mena. Good. Better to pray with a holy man than alone.

But is he holy just for being Haji? Anwar shook his head in consternation, touched the scabs on his face, and managed a shrug. "How long have you fought in this holy war?"

"Forever. Did you not see the gray in my beard? And you? But never mind, for I see the answer written upon your clothing, upon the weapon you think is yours, upon the way you walk. Days. You have been in the war only days, and combat is new, and you have never watched a man die because of what you have done with your hands and with a weapon made in some foreign land. I know you, for you are a younger version of me, a man not unlike my son, and I know you think you would die gladly in the war against the Great Satan. But would you? I think not, at least not without a nudge, and I think we both doubt you would attain heaven in the instance of that nudge, in spite of what the recruiters say. You, too, have doubts, I know. Here. The flat rocks. You must perform the ablution."

"That would be nice." Anwar thought the man joked, for where could there be water on dry rocks? Some men performed the religious washing with sand, rubbing hands, arms, face, and feet with powder that drifted in the breeze, settled as dirt. This was no holy washing, Anwar concluded. When it wasn't possible to wash, then the faithful prayed anyway. Sand and dirt could never be a substitute. Anwar looked around, struck by the thought that Abu Hassan might mean they should rub themselves with soil.

But no, Anwar saw with relief. Abu Hassan produced a plastic bottle from beneath his shirt, a capped bottle that once held a dark sugary drink favored by Americans but now held a bit of murky water. He shook his head as in apology. "Not enough for us both, but for you, here. I'll pour, and the washing will be more symbol than actual. Give me your hands."

With sleeves pulled past elbows, Anwar submitted to the sprinkling, recoiling at the odor. "This is not water."

"No. Not entirely. Vinegar, some of it, but I took what I could find for ablution, and what I found was a jug of vinegar. It will work, though not so well as water."

Anwar splashed his face, winced at the smell of vinegar, and sat to remove his shoes. "This is not water."

"My son once complained because all we had was desert sand for the ablution. It was our final prayer together, for he died soon after, died in this bloody war, and I have regretted not finding water for him. It has been six weeks now, or so I believe, for the days run together, and I can gauge time only by the coming of cool wind."

"Your son died a martyr, then. I'm sorry and I am glad."

"Not me. I'm sorry, only sorry. It goes against the natural order, this dying of a son before his father. I didn't know earlier in the war, but have learned through loss."

"He attained heaven."

"Take this, and take my apologies for this weak ablution, for the stink of vinegar to disrupt your prayers. The last for your feet." Abu Hassan emptied the bottle in Anwar's cupped hands. "Pray now, and say short suras, for the chill of night comes fast, and you must cover your feet." He looked again at the sky, and Anwar thought the man became tense. "If it comes while you are at prayer, jump into that gully. There is no merit in dying just to die. Always remember that you must save yourself. You must."

"If what comes?"

"The bomb."

"Will you not pray with me?"

"I will return to the mosque to fill the bottle with good water, and I will bring it to you." He turned to go.

"But what if the bomb comes while you're there?" The man is more than a bit crazy, Anwar thought, going toward such a target.

Abu Hassan walked on without answering, one arm hugging his ribs, and Anwar began chanting his first sura.

He had almost finished praying when the whistle of the bomb announced its coming. Anwar scrambled into the gully, put his hands over his head, and endured the concussion, feeling his ears become numb, moist, and his nose bleed. He crawled to the ridge of the rock and looked at the burning mosque giving light enough to reveal the destruction of the tanks and trucks. The Pashtun and their foolishness did that, he thought. They had no regard at all for the mosque or for the likes of Abu Hassan, who was kind, Anwar told himself, even in his lunacy.

Red Pickup

Joel chased the grasshopper across the vacant lot next door and into old man Bentley's yard. Terri carried the jar and stayed right behind her younger brother. She worried that he would fall and hit that spot on his head again, so she didn't see Bentley until it was too late.

"You little snots get outta my yard," Bentley snapped. He stood in a flower bed, waving a rake in a threatening way. Terri stopped and stared, wide-eyed.

Joel continued after the grasshopper. When it landed, he slapped it with his stuffed snake. The grasshopper opened its wings and quivered. Joel picked it up, glanced at Bentley, and walked back to Terri. "It ain't dead," he said. "It's spitting up that brown stuff. Tobacco juice."

Terri retreated and Joel followed. "Open the jar, and I'll drop her in," Joel said.

"That old man scared me." Terri opened the jar and Joel dropped the grasshopper inside.

"Me, too."

"You didn't look scared. I think maybe I wet my pants a little bit when he hollered."

Joel looked startled, then laughed.

Terri liked it that Joel laughed. He didn't seem to do that much anymore. Not that Terri could blame him, seeing as how every time Daddy came around, Mama sent her and Joel outside.

"Grown-up talk?" Joel had asked. He picked up his stuffed snake and headed for the door without waiting for an answer.

When Terri got outside, she found him sitting by the porch, the snake hanging around his neck. He stared at the red pickup truck on the ground in front of him. She sat beside him and examined the place on his head that he seemed to hit every time he fell down.

"I got a mayonnaise jar with holes punched in the top," she said. "You want to catch some grasshoppers and go fishing?"

"Daddy said it looks just like his new truck. And it does. Just like it. Ain't that right?" Joel nudged the toy truck with his foot.

"Not exactly. Both are red. Yours is a little smaller."

"Exactly alike. Exactly."

'What about the grasshoppers? You want to go fishing or what?"

"In Alligator Bayou?" Joel pushed the truck again.

"Can't do that. Mama said so. The bayou is too far out and too deep. But we can go to the cattail pond."

"Daddy says there's no bass there. Daddy says the bass live in the bayou. Only little bitsy perch live in the pond on account of it's so shallow."

"So do we go or what?"

"We dig worms for bait?"

"No. I want to try some grasshoppers this time. If you can catch them." Terri said it like she knew Joel couldn't catch a grasshopper if he tried.

Joel picked up the truck and put it into his pocket. "I can catch a hundred of them," he had said. "more than your jar can hold. More than you can carry."

When they got to the pond Joel unwound the string from the fishing pole. "I'll stick the bug on the hook."

Terry held up the jar and examined the grasshopper. Its wings looked like tiny leaves. "You caught it real sneaky. I never thought you would hit it with your snake." She looked at the brown juice globbed on the grasshopper's mouth. Maybe Joel ought to be the one to stick the fishhook into the grasshopper, she thought. But what if he stuck himself? He seemed to be having a lot of accidents lately.

"Snakes eat grasshoppers." Joel pushed the snake's head against the jar and made munching sounds. "And rats. Daddy said snakes like to eat rats. I would eat a rat, if I could catch one. I would hit it with the snake wham wham. Then crack it open and eat it."

"Gross. Joel, that's gross." She opened the jar.

"I get to fish first." Joel thrust his hand inside and grabbed the grasshopper. "Then you fish. And when we don't get a single bite, we go down to Alligator Bayou and fish."

Terri sat on the bank and watched Joel stick the fishhook into the grasshopper. It squirmed and produced more tobacco juice. Joel adjusted the depth of the red plastic bobber, picked up the pole and swung it so the grasshopper landed in the water.

As soon as the line hit the water, the bass struck. Terri jumped to her feet. Joel remained calm. He let the fish run for a few seconds, then lifted the pole to set the hook.

The pole bent, and the line cut the water with a ripping sound. Joel lifted the pole, jerking the fish out of the water. He held it dancing on the end of the string for a long moment, looking open-mouthed at the size of it. As he swung the bass over the bank, the fish dropped from the hook, landed on the grass and flopped about.

"Grab it," Joel said. "Grab it. Keep it out of the water."

The bass stopped flopping for a moment. Terri and Joel approached it with hesitation. With a suddenness that shocked Terri, the bass flounced back into the water. She had to catch the back of Joel's shirt to keep him from wading in after it. He stood for moment, leaning against her hold on his shirt, then jerked away.

"I'm glad it got back into the pond," Terri said.

Joel sat down with startling abruptness. He picked up a rock and looked at it with an intense frown.

She was about to say something when she heard Daddy call. Joel looked up, the frown falling away. "Hear that? That's Daddy." He threw the rock into the pond. "Let's go see Daddy."

Daddy hadn't been staying at home much, and Terri knew why. It was because she had disappointed him in some way. She kept her room too messy, or she used to before Daddy started spending the night away from home. Was that what she had done to make Daddy not like her anymore? She didn't know, but she did understand that Daddy was grumpy when he was around her. Terri felt unsure of the nature of her crime, but she knew she was to blame for Daddy's wanting to be somewhere other than in his home.

In the living room Terri saw that whatever Daddy was unhappy about had gotten worse. Mama's cheeks were flushed, and Daddy looked grim. Joel didn't seem to notice, though. He went up to Daddy and held out his hand. "Gimme five," he said.

"Joel," Mama said, "you and Terri sit down. We need to talk."

"I caught a bass." Joel spread his arms as wide as he could. "This big. Bigger."

"That's fine, " Mama said. "Terri, do you and Joel know what *divorce* means?"

"It got away. But it was this big."

"Not to live together anymore?" Terri felt a heavy lump come into her stomach. Joel dropped his arms. He sat down in the middle of the floor.

Terri saw that terrible frown come back to knit his brows in a scary way. She wanted to say something to him, but she didn't. She sat by Daddy and tried to figure out how to tell him she was sorry for doing whatever it was that made him want to go away.

"Your daddy and I have talked it over, and we think it best if he and I get a divorce. He will move to an apartment, and you and me and Joel will live here, same as always."

"I don't like that." Terri tried to keep from crying. "I don't want you to do that."

Joel got up and began digging in his pocket. Mama and Daddy sat in silence while Terri folded her arms across her breast and sniffed.

"Joel," Mama said, "do you understand what I just said?"

"Yes. That Daddy's going to go away." He danced about, jerking at something stuck in a pocket.

"He won't go far. And he'll come to visit you on weekends."

Joel pulled the red pickup from a pocket and waved it around. "Will you still have your truck? The one just exactly like this one?"

"Yes, Joel," Mama said. "Your daddy will keep the truck."

"Then, then," Joel whirled around and strode to the door. He stopped and looked back. "Then everything is all right." He went outside.

"Yeah," Daddy said, his voice sounding flat and strange to Terri. "Everything is just fine and dandy."

"Terri," Mama said, "we need to talk more about all this, you and me. And Joel, too. But right now, you just run along, okay? Go check on your little brother."

Terri wiped away a tear with a quick gesture so they wouldn't see. She went outside.

From the porch, she saw Joel heading toward the cattail pond. Gone back to catch that big bass, she thought. He doesn't even understand, not at all. But then how could he know that his sister caused Daddy and Mama to want to get a divorce? And if Joel did know, Terri was sure he would hate her.

She wandered off the path, swishing her shoes through the weeds. When she got close to the pond, she could see Joel was busy with something on the ground. He seemed to be pounding on something. Maybe, Terri thought, he caught a rat and he's trying to crack it open. She figured he'd be silly enough to try to eat it. She quickened her pace.

When she got closer and saw the toy truck, she stopped. Joel hammered at it with a rock, knocking flecks of red from it. Two of its wheels lay a few feet away.

84

Joel gave the toy a final blow with the rock and kicked the truck into the pond. He sat for a moment, watching the bubbles where it sank, then began pounding on his head with the rock.

Blood gushed across his forehead, but Joel kept at it, hammering with the same mechanical motion he had used on the truck. Terri began running toward him. "Joel, Joel," she said, her voice high and thin.

El Don and the Bandits

"Don, Don, the piper's son," El Loco said. "Stole a pig and away he run. Or was it Tom? And was he blond like you?" He took a swig of the *Lava Gallo* whiskey and broke into song: "Maresey doats and doesey doats, maresey doats and doesey doats for chrissake." He sat up straight, almost hitting his head on the machete Rosita had stuck in the tree. "Listen. Horses. That means only one thing—the effing bandits are coming to collect taxes. News seems to travel fast around here, when it comes to gold."

"He's talking in English again." Rosita rolled her eyes. "What did he say?"

"He said he hears horses." The locals were right to call the man *el loco*, I thought, even if he did give us food. Rosita and I had been separated from the truck that abandoned us in the wild part of Venezuela for only a day, but that was long enough to feel the pinch of hunger.

El Loco stood and glanced around. "The savannah," he said in Spanish. "You two get over there where the grass is highest and thickest. Hide in the savannah and don't make a sound. Those men are bad." He began shoving us toward the thick wall of savannah grass at the edge of his camp. "They would probably kill you, Don, and they might do terrible things to Rosita."

"Kill?" Rosita said in disbelief.

"Yes. Get in there now. Fast. Lie down and make no noise at all, no matter what you hear the bandits do."

We parted the grasses and stepped into them. El Loco pushed the grass back into shape as we mashed enough of it around us to lie down. He retreated, kicking the sand to cover our footprints.

"I hear the horses now," Rosita said. "That man has ears like a jackass."

El Loco turned the bottle up. I could see bubbles rise in the bottle and imagined that I heard it gurgle. Then the horses thundered into the camp,

87

kicking up dust. "Five horses," I whispered. "And look, there's Carlos, that nasty man we saw at the cantina."

"Hush." Rosita nudged me with her elbow.

"Good day to you, El Loco Merzi," the lead rider said. He rode, as all the men did, barebacked, holding reins, and he looked like an ordinary man with a moustache. I was a little disappointed that he didn't carry a rifle and have cartridges of bullets slung across his shoulders. There was a pistol sticking out from his belt, and the sight of it gave me a thrill. The men dismounted and handed their reins to a pock-marked fellow who was small enough to pass for a boy. The pock-marked man seemed nervous, and as soon as he had the reins of the horses, he began edging out of the camp.

Mr. Moustache turned to him and demanded in a querulous voice, "Where are you going?"

"The bad luck doll," the man muttered, making the sign against the evil eye.

"Ha," Mr. Moustache said. "Sometimes El Loco isn't so loco." He took the pistol from his belt and fired at the doll hanging from the chaparro tree. The doll jumped and bounced around on the chord that held it in the tree. "It's evil eye is now dead."

A look of relief spread across the face of the pock-marked man, and he stopped making the sign against the evil eye.

Mr. Moustache turned to El Loco. "I heard you struck it rich," he said.

"Did I do that?" El Loco looked amazed. "I didn't know. It's good news, though, for now I can retire, move to a ranch in California, and have many servants. Perhaps I should start packing up the gold that I didn't know I had. Can you tell me where to find it?"

The men laughed. "He has gold," Carlos said. "I saw a chunk of it the size of my fist."

"Yes. So you claim," Mr. Moustache said. "The nugget grows every time you tell the story. Now shut up. Juan, get the small bit of gold from his tent."

The one called Juan crawled into the pup tent. El Loco took another swig from his bottle, and Mr. Moustache paced around, looking at the ground as if he expected to find chunks of gold everywhere. El Loco began a slow shuffle toward his campfire. Juan emerged from the tent holding a piece of cloth tied with a string. "It feels like very little," he said.

"That's all I have this time, and I'm telling the truth," El Loco said, edging closer to the campfire and glancing at it.

"If that's all you have, then I'm a bunch of radish," Mr. Moustache said. He watched El Loco with care. "Juan, look inside that pot hanging over the burnt sticks."

El Loco seemed to brighten. "Maybe Juan could wash the pot for me when he checks it for gold? Here, I'll get it for him." El Loco took the pot from the wire hook tied to a branch in the chaparro tree above my machete, still stuck in the tree from Rosita's swinging the machete when she was angry with El Loco.

"Look," Juan said. "A machete stuck in the tree. What is the meaning of that?" He took the handle of the machete and jerked on it. "It seems to be grown into the tree, *carumba*." He jerked on the handle a few more times.

"Leave the machete alone, *pendejo*. Look in the pot like I told you," Mr. Moustache said.

El Loco handed off the pot, then retreated to the burned-out campfire. Mr. Moustache s looked at the remains of the campfire. "Juan. Get a shovel."

"There's nothing in the pot but dried pieces of bread," Juan said.

"I know. Get a shovel and dig where the fire was."

Juan looked around, spied a shovel leaning against the box down by the stream, and headed for it.

"No." El Loco became alarmed. "It is bad luck to dig there. The person who digs there will get warts on his face. The dead fire has been cursed. Anyone who digs it up and looks into the hole won't be able to pee for a month."

"*Carajo*." The pock-marked man moved back and made the sign against the evil eye.

"This was easier than usual," Mr. Moustache said. He turned to Carlos. "I hope there's enough gold to make our trip here worth my time."

"I do wish you wouldn't dig up my campfire," El Loco whined.

Juan returned with the shovel and started excavating the campfire. The third shovel of dirt unearthed something, and Juan dropped to his knees. "This is large and heavy," he said.

Mr. Moustache pushed Juan aside and plucked a piece of tied-up cloth from the hole. He shook dirt from the bundle. "It is larger than usual, but not so heavy." He ripped the cloth and dumped some stones onto the ground. "Bah." He nudged the stones with the toe of his boot. "Pick them up, Juan. There's some gold in them, but they're mostly just rocks. Carlos."

"It took me months to dig that little bit of gold out of the hard ground," El Loco said. "Leave the gold stones for me. Leave half of them for me. Isn't my labor worth something?"

"You bought whiskey with my gold," Mr. Moustache said. "I'll leave you the *Lava Gallo* as payment. Only a man with a stomach made of rock can drink such a brew."

"He also bought flour, salt, and beans," Carlos ventured. "You could take that."

"And have my servant starve? Don't be a fool."

"Leave me just one of the gold stones," El Loco pleaded.

"Maybe he gave some of his gold to the children I told you about," Carlos said. "Maybe he is supplying El Don with gold for weapons to arm the peasants."

"El Don." Mr. Moustache spat on the ground. "Where do you get such stupid ideas? I killed El Don when he cheated me in a card game."

"His son, the new El Don. That's who I mean. I saw him. He has golden hair and skin white as a fish's belly."

"Shut up. There is no son." Mr. Moustache turned to El Loco. "You stupid old man, you worked for how long since I last visited you? Three months? Four? And you barely dug enough gold for me to have a meal and a night with a whore. You must stop pushing that wheelbarrow all over the place and dig only where you find gold. Juan, get the rocks. My horse, where is my horse? I've had enough of crazy people. Carlos, if you play such a trick on me again, I will feed your *plátano* to the cannibal fish."

The men mounted and rode away. El Loco took another drink of *Lava Gallo* and laughed. "A kiddledy divy too, wouldn't you?" he sang as he stumbled toward the chaparro tree. "What, ho?" He tried to kick the machete, but he couldn't kick that high. "A bare bodkin. Shit." He sat down and leaned against the tree. "They're all gone, all the bad horses and all the bad men who can't put all the gold together again. El Don and La Doña Rosita can now come out of the grass."

"Are we safe?" I asked.

"I think so," Rosita said. "Let's go ask Mr. Jackass Ears about El Don."

"Jackass Ears?" El Loco laughed. "I like that name. You are to call me that from now on."

We stood and brushed the dust and grass from us. "Why is he so jolly?" I asked. "The bandits just took all his gold."

"Hush, Don." We approached El Loco.

"You said you wouldn't tell me that again."

"All my gold, alas. *Todo.* Every bit. Each flake. Every nugget and all the rocks that glittered, goddam, leaving me destitute, poorer than a church mouse, broke as last year's toothpicks, flat as fungus, and without funds, shoot."

"What did he say?"

"He said something about a mouse and some toothpicks. It sounded like nonsense to me."

"Right on, young man, heir to the throne, the Don of the Oronocco, Prince of Dust Devils, and King of the black *caimanes.* All of my words are nonsense. That's why the people wisely call me El Loco. To you, however, I am now Jackass Ears. You may call me Mister Jackass or Mister Ears, as you like."

"Don't ask," I told Rosita. "I didn't understand that speech at all."

Color rose in Rosita's cheeks. "You will talk only Spanish. Please tell us why everyone thinks Don is El Don."

"I am stricken," El Loco said in Spanish. "The bandits take all my gold, and all you can do is to lecture me about how to talk."

"You have plenty of gold hidden elsewhere." Rosita put her hands on her hips and stepped closer to El Loco. "And if you cannot remember where you hid it, then you can find more in the gully beneath the chaparro tree, where you push your wheelbarrow at night."

El Loco stared at her, open-mouthed.

"We watched you while we sat in the tree by the gully."

"Don't talk about that gully," El Loco said in a harsh whisper. He cleared his throat and smiled. "Please sit down and I'll tell you some stories. I'll even answer your question, but you must be patient, for my head is spinning with *Lava Gallo.* Sit. Sit."

As we sat, I asked Rosita, "What did you mean about more gold? The bandits took all he had, we saw that."

"Hush, Don."

"You told me you wouldn't say that."

"I'm sorry." She turned to me and put her hand on mine. "I truly am sorry."

She looked so contrite that I shrugged and said, "Forget it."

"Thank you, Don, my good friend." Rosita patted my hand and turned her attention to El Loco. When she did, her face hardened. "Stop drinking so you can make sense when you talk. Who is El Don?"

El Loco looked limp and shapeless as a piece of chewed sugarcane. He took a defiant swig from the bottle. "Dead, that's who he is. Deader than a doornail. Deader than last week's belch or the dreams of youth. Deader than a mackerel. I wish I had a mackerel right now. I'd eat that sumbitch without salt. Goddam." He took another drink.

"What did he say?" Rosita nudged me.

"He said El Don is dead and that he wants to eat some fish without salt."

"That's no help. Stop drinking now, El Loco. And please remember that I don't understand English." She offered to take the bottle from him.

He clutched it to his breast. "No you don't, sweetheart." He glanced at the machete. "And you please keep in mind that I ain't flirting. Saying sweetheart is just a manner of talking. And little laaaambsey divy."

"Stop that silly singing and talk to me in Spanish, you drunk goat," Rosita snapped.

"Bueno. Spanish it is," El Loco said.

I was relieved that he switched languages. "What will the bandits do," I asked, "if I try to get my land back?" Rosita shot me a sharp look, and I expected her to tell me to be quiet, but she didn't.

"Does it matter what you try to do? Not at all. You are not in control of anything—nobody is." El Loco shook the bottle at Rosita. "Not even you, sweet princess of swinging machetes and queen of the curled lip. Nothing you try to do makes any difference, even if you must try to force your life to be the way you want. The bandits are also puppets. We are all poor players in a game with dim rules we don't know about. We work and sweat and kill and die, and nothing we do changes what we will do." As he spoke, his voice became lower, and he looked to be on the edge of tears. "That goddam Chinaman was right. By doing nothing, everything gets accomplished. But I can't just sit and do nothing. I can't—even if what I do doesn't matter."

"I think he is crazy," Rosita said.

"Children and drunkards tell the truth," El Loco said.

"What about my land?" I asked.

"You have no land. You're just a boy. A good one, though, suckering Mamacita Moreno with that chunk of gold rock and getting her for two bottles. Two." He took a drink and continued in a slurred voice: "They'll be here, those boys from Maracaibo, soon as they get a sniff of my gold. They'll follow me around for days, the stupid goats. I won't be able to go near my gold mine for weeks, maybe. You know what those goats do? They watch me dig, then they go dig like crazy men, straight down, finding nothing because there's nothing where I dig." He laughed. "I let them work like Chinamen, then I go dig somewhere else, and they follow and dig there. Wears them out, and they call me crazy for digging all over the place. Soon as they give up, I get back to digging where the gold is, but only in the dead of the night when those lazy goats are at the cantina with Mamacita's women. Won't none of them come into my camp on account of my bad luck doll with the evil eye, heh, heh, heh." He glanced at the doll and frowned. "The stinking son of a goat shot my hex doll, goddam."

"The men from Maracaibo and the bandits keep you busy," Rosita said.

"The bandits, yes. Those guys don't care about my doll, mostly. They march right into camp to collect taxes. I pay them, too, but not as much as they might get if they weren't so stupid. And why the hell is Carmencita la Gatita hanging around my camp?" He pointed with the neck of the bottle.

The one-eyed lady we had seen washing clothes stood on the trail, making little jerky motions with one hand, holding the other out in front of her.

"Why did you call her Carmen the cat?" I asked.

"She's making the sign that guards against the evil eye," Rosita said, then glanced at the doll hanging from the other chaparro.

"She has only one eye, and I have the evil eye hanging in the tree," El Loco said in English. "It keeps the goddam superstitious natives out of my camp. Except for the bandit tax collectors, of course." He then switched to Spanish and raised his voice as Rosita headed for the other chaparro tree: "You leave that doll alone."

"I will not." Rosita climbed the chaparro fast as a monkey and got the doll. She shinnied down the tree and threw the doll into El Loco's tent. Only then would the one-eyed lady come into the camp.

"Carmen, beautiful and once beloved Carmen," El Loco said. "Though you paint an inch thick, you must come to this."

The one-eyed lady kept casting sidelong glances at the pup tent as she entered the camp. "Why is there a machete in the chaparro?" She grabbed the handle and pulled the machete away from the tree.

"*Madre de Dios,*" Rosita said.

"Goddam," El Loco said. "None of us could pull that out after Rosita stuck it there."

"Juan must have loosened it," I said.

El Loco closed one eye and looked over the neck of the bottle at me as if he were aiming a pistol. "Don't say such a thing, Don. Don't even think it. Life is too hard without magic, and what Carmen did just now is magic as sure as butterflies ain't made of butter." He turned his attention to Carmen. "You are of royal blood, that's clear. You are the princess of the Savannah and heir to the kingdom of El Don."

"How much has he drunk?" Carmen asked me.

"Nearly half a bottle of *Lava Gallo*. But he didn't make much sense before he started drinking."

"Out of the mouths of babes," El Loco said in English.

"Speak so I can understand, please," Carmen said.

"He might for a while, but he likes to talk to Don in their language," Rosita said.

"Yeah," I said, "and the words he says might as well be in German."

"Don't listen to him," Carmen said. "It is you, El Don, who is important here. You must reclaim your land."

"El Loco says I have no land, and he's right. I'm just a boy from El Tigrito who was stranded here by the candy man. Ask Rosita."

"That might be true. But it is also true that you are now El Don. I believe it. The people who worked for the old Don believe it because I told them about you and your golden hair. Even the ruined men from Maracaibo believe it. Like it or not, you are now El Don."

"Believing it doesn't make it true."

"No, El Don, you're wrong. Believing is the only thing that makes something true. And now that you are a man of much importance, you must help the people who know you and love you and believe in you."

"Goddam," El Loco said in surprise. "That's pretty damn profound for a one-eyed whore."

"I asked you not to speak in English," Carmen said. "What did he say, El Don?"

"I think he said you're right."

"I am right. Now you must hear my plan."

"We need to go home," Rosita said.

"Hush, child. You are the servant of El Don. It is your duty to help him do what he must do. You will stand behind El Don when he tells the people to rise against the bandits and kill them. Look at me. I was once young and beautiful and could see from two eyes so brown that I broke men's hearts. I broke his heart," she pointed at El Loco. "Then the bandits slashed me with a knife, cut my face into ugliness, and killed the fire in my eye."

"You seem to have rediscovered some of the fire in your head," El Loco said.

"Yes. And if you had any sense, you would look with your heart beyond my empty socket and scars. But, El Don, ignore him, the stupid goat. The bandits killed your father and butchered your cattle and even now live in the home that your father built."

"My father lives in El Tigrito, and I was there until yesterday."

"Perhaps. But your father is also dead and I am wounded and ugly, and for what? So the bandits can have the land that gave a good life to many good people. The people are afraid of the bad men, afraid of dying or being mutilated the way the bandits mutilated me. So they do nothing. But if you talk to them, it will give them hope."

"Why me?"

"Because of your golden hair. Because of your age. Because you are now El Don. The old Don had a boy with golden hair. He would be about your age now, but the bandits say they shot him and buried him with his father."

"Then I am not El Don."

"Don't argue with her, boy," El Loco said. "You'll lose. Never argue with a woman who has a fire in her head."

"Listen to this man," Carmen said. "He speaks the truth."

"But you told me not to listen to him."

"You're arguing with her again." El Loco said. "Now you know why I called her a cat. Have you ever been able to argue with a cat and win?"

"The people are gathering down by the small river. You will come with me and speak to them."

"No I won't. You want me to tell some people to kill some other people. Miss Carmen, I couldn't even kill an iguana if I were starving."

"It's true," Rosita said, "about the iguana."

"Do you value your servant girl?" Carmen asked.

"Rosita is my best friend. She is not my servant." It surprised me to hear myself calling her my best friend, but I knew it was true as I spoke. Rosita looked at me, her eyes rounded in wonder, then she gave me a solemn nod.

"Good enough." Carmen sighed. "I do wish you would come without my having to do this." She turned and called out, "Simón, come get these unruly children." A man wearing khakis and boots emerged from the savannah grass. He held a pistol, and he smiled in a mean-looking way. Dark, sinister-looking brows slanted into a frown and almost met over his nose, and his cheeks were thin and leathery. A white gash of a scar ran through his moustache, giving him the appearance of snarling. "Simón, if El Don doesn't obey me, shoot the girl."

"No." I leaped to my feet and snatched the machete from her.

"Get back," Simón said, pointing the pistol at me. "Get back."

"Goddam," El Loco said. "So much for romance. So much for this whore being of royal blood."

"Speak Spanish, you goat-licker," Carmen said. "El Don, you will take the machete by the blade and hand it to me. Your friend is beautiful, even as I once was. It would be a shame if she came to harm."

I handed her the machete. Rosita took my arm and stood close to me.

"And you, you crazy old man. Stand up." As El Loco struggled to his feet, Carmen snatched the bottle from him and threw it down. The whiskey gurgled out and vanished into the dry sand.

"Goddam," El Loco said.

"I loved you once. Did you know that?"

El Loco looked as if someone had struck him in the stomach. "Don't say it. Don't say such cruel things to an old man." He burst into tears.

Rosita went to him, patted his back, and said, "It's hard to be loved in such a way. I know. Crying helps."

"Shut up both of you," Carmen said, her voice husky.

The man with the pistol looked confused, and he began to blot his eyes on his shirt sleeve as he looked from El Loco to Carmen. The corners of his mouth turned down, his fierce eyebrows wilted into misery, and he began to blubber. He sniffed a couple of times, put his thumb over one nostril and blew a mist out of the other, then said in a voice that cracked, "We need to go. The people will be waiting, and look. Rain comes."

El Loco wiped a tear from his cheek. "That was bygod gross, Simón," he said.

"Yes, rain," Carmen said. "We are lucky, for it looks as if it will rain as the day falls into night. But look at you. What a bunch of babies—all of you crying except for El Don, who is the best man here." Carmen whacked El Loco's bottom with the flat side of the machete. "March. And be assured that was the last time I ever tell a man that I once loved him. El Don, you come walk beside me. Simón, walk behind the other two, and keep your pistol ready. I don't trust El Loco because he is loco, and I don't trust the children because they are children. Shoot them if they try to run away, but shoot them in the legs."

As we left the savannah to walk among the long shadows of palms, giant rosewood, and mango trees, I said, "Miss Carmen, I won't tell anyone to kill anyone else."

"I know. It's because you have a good heart. Say only a few words. I'll tell you what those words are."

When she told me, I was surprised. "That's all?"

"Yes. Doing the right thing is easy, El Don, once you know what it is."

"Maresey doats and doesey doats and little laaaambsey die-vey," El Loco sang. I thought his voice sounded more sober than it did back in his camp and that it had a sad note in it.

As we moved deeper into the jungle, night came on, and the noises of the night creatures began. We walked past something with a scary bass voice said a single word: "Ralph. Ralph. Ralph." A million insects began buzzing and clicking, and whistle frogs added to the din with a continuous chorus of single high-pitched notes.

We rounded a bend in the path into a clearing beside the river, and I saw that Carmen was right—it wasn't a big river at all. Ground palms with fronds as large as those in the tall palm trees grew along the edge of the water. Though it was hard to make out in the shadows of twilight, I saw a canoe tied to a bush. Beyond the canoe stood a little shack of a house and several lighted kerosene lanterns suspended on poles. Beside the shack two groups of men milled about. The large group—fifteen or twenty—wore rough cotton pants and shirts similar to those worn by the natives in El Tigrito, along with simple *apagatos* instead of leather boots or shoes. The other group seemed better dressed, but they looked much dirtier. I figured these were the men from Maracaibo who came to the wild part of Venezuela in search of gold. As we walked into the clearing, both groups stirred and the buzzing of their talk turned to silence, and I again became aware of the night sounds of the jungle.

Carmen pushed me forward and said, "Men, I present to you El Don." The poorer men wearing *apagatos* cheered, and the men in boots made subdued noises of approval. "Talk to them," Carmen prompted. I felt jittery and wasn't sure I could talk without my voice cracking, so I spent some time clearing my throat. "Now," Carmen said in a harsh whisper.

"You are men of men," I said. "You know what is the right thing to do, and I support you in doing it."

The men waited for more, but that was all Carmen had told me to say. One of the men asked, "Will you make the land rich again, as your father did?"

"Now," Carmen whispered to me, "you will shut up." She walked among the men speaking in a shrill voice: "You heard El Don. He is only a boy and already he is a man of judgment. Go. All of you. Kill the bandits. Take their ill-gotten gold, and return our land to prosperity once again. Go now. Night falls and rain comes. The bandits have grown fat and lazy. They think you are all women, that you have no spines, so they will not suspect that you will fall upon them. Take your pistols, those who have any. Take your shotguns. Take your knives and machetes," she waved my machete around over her head, "and rush them just after the rain starts to pound upon the roof. They will not hear you come upon them because of the rain. They will not suspect anyone of attacking them on such a night. I will stay here to keep El Don safe. Return when the scourge of our land lies bleeding and dead in the very house where they once butchered El Don, the father of this young Don. Now. Go in stealth; go with heavy hearts; go knowing justice is on your side; and go knowing there is gold in the pockets of the bandits, gold that now belongs to you."

This time the men from Maracaibo cheered along with the others. Then they all rushed back down the trail we had used. Within minutes only Rosita, Carmen, El Loco and I were left standing in the flickering light of the kerosene lamps.

"Those men are going to kill others. That's wrong," I said.

"Maybe," El Loco said in Spanish. "Maybe not. For sure it isn't right that the bandits killed the old Don and took his house. It isn't right that they stole the eye of the one woman I ever loved and made her turn from me and all men in bitterness."

"I turn from you?" Carmen said. "You abandoned me because I was ugly and because all you cared about was gold."

"I dug gold only for you." El Loco raised his voice. "I pretended to be crazy to keep gold thieves from taking me seriously—I pretended until perhaps I became a little crazy. For you, Carmencita, I dug gold—remember what you told me? That you would never have a man who was as poor as I was? You sent me away. Then I dug gold from habit, because there was nothing more for me to do."

"Liar," Carmen whispered and started crying. "Liar. Liar." She dropped my machete and put her hands over her face.

El Loco put an arm around her. "Yes. I have learned to tell lies," he said, then dropped his voice to a whisper. They wandered toward the shack, absorbed in each other, ignoring us.

"This is not a good place for us to be," Rosita said.

"Then let's leave. Maybe we can stand under one of those palms when the rain comes."

"No. We take the canoe." Rosita pointed toward the small river. It was so dark I could barely make out the shape of the bush where the canoe was tied.

"My machete," I said, picking it up. As soon as I had it in my hand I remembered the wheelbarrow putting blisters below my fingers.

"Yes," Rosita said, her voice full of excitement. "Cut some palm fronds from the palmettoes. We will use them for umbrellas when we're in the canoe." She led me to the canoe, which wasn't like any I had ever seen. The sides pinched in toward the bottom, giving it the shape of a canoe. But the bottom was flat and much wider than I expected. "Get the palm fronds." She began untying the rope from the bush.

I poked around the dark masses of palm fronds and hacked at them until I had a stack of large ones. Swinging the machete wasn't fun because of the sore places on my hands. The wind picked up as I put the palms into the canoe.

"Get in, quick," Rosita said. "Before someone stops us."

"We're going to steal the boat?"

"Not steal. Borrow. Besides, I think the boat belongs to Carmen, and she owes us for telling Simón to shoot us if we didn't obey her."

"It's still stealing." The canoe didn't tip much when I stepped into it. "Do you have paddles?" I asked.

"Yes. Sit down so we can get going."

I settled into the bottom of the canoe and felt water soak into my pants. "I'm sitting in water," I said.

"Stop whining. So am I. Here, take this paddle. No, put down your machete first. Take it, and let's get going."

"Which direction?"

"There's only one direction we can go. With the flow of the river. Now be quiet and help me. I'll guide because I'm in the back. You watch for rocks and logs."

At that moment a clap of lightening roared overhead, giving me a brief view of the jungle around us. Vines hung everywhere, and trees leaned into the water. Then the rain began, and I tried to shelter my head with a palm frond.

It was impossible to hold both the palm and the paddle, so I gave up and decided it was fine to get soaked. The rain felt cool, almost cold, and I knew that before the night was over it would be quite cool. Turns in the narrow river caused leaves to drag across the canoe, across my face. It was necessary to keep ducking and, from time to time, to use the paddle to push us away from the shore. Rain kept falling, making a hissing sound in the water and on the trees of the jungle. More thunder sounded, but there was no lightening. "Gunfire," Rosita said. "Not far away."

She was right; the sounds were not thunder. We heard only three or four blasts from shotguns and a few popping noises from pistols, then heard only the hiss of the rain. "Some men are now dead that were breathing just a few minutes ago," I said.

We flowed with the river, avoiding talking, ducking under overhanging trees and paddling to stay in the center. Then I said: "It is my fault."

"No," Rosita said. The hiss of rain quieted and stopped. Drops plopped into the water from trees, the river water gurgled against the bank, and wet leaves kept brushing us. Then there were no more leaves to push aside and we couldn't hear the sound of water against the riverbank. Overhead, clouds parted to reveal the brilliance of the stars. "The river," Rosita said.

"I think the river ran into a lake," I said. "We should find a place to go ashore and dry off before we get too cold."

"It would be dangerous to go into a strange jungle at night. We must stay in the boat until daylight. I found a can for dipping out the water." I heard the scraping sound as she scooped water from the bottom of the canoe, then heard the splash of her emptying the can overboard.

"It wasn't your fault."

"But it is."

"No. The bandits killed your father. I mean the father of the other blond boy. They robbed the peasants. They robbed El Loco. It isn't your fault that the peasants and the men from Maracaibo killed them."

"Maybe the bandits killed the men who attacked them. That would mean I sent them there to die."

"I think not. There were too few gunshots for the bandits to have stayed alive. All of them had guns, and few of the peasants and gold-seekers had guns, remember? I think the battle was fought mostly with machetes and knives. That means the good people won."

"Is it wrong to kill bad people?"

"No. Yes. I don't know. But I do know that it would happen sooner or later—the peasants would cut the throats of those who had cheated them of a good life. You had nothing to do with it."

"Yes I did. I told them I supported what they were going to do."

"But you didn't tell them what to do."

"No." I thought she was right about that. Carmen told them what to do, so she was bad, then, and not I. It relieved me some to shift the blame to Carmen. "Carmen said believing something makes it true. Do you believe that?"

Rosita yawned. "I don't know. Yes. Ask me in the morning. Don, I'm wet and cold and sitting in an uncomfortable boat. But for all that, this is a good hour, for we're somewhere in a wonderful jungle lake." She sighed. "I love the jungle," and her voice trailed off to vanish in the sounds of night insects and frogs.

Firethorn Arch

Drusilla backed away from Hank, moving from the cabinet, from the Frydaddy that snapped and popped potatoes to the golden brown Hank demanded. She knew he liked her to cringe, that it stoked the fires that burned him into drawing his fingers into fists the size of sledgehammers; she knew that her cringing made him want to slam those fists into her face, her body. But she couldn't help backing away, moving to the edge of the pantry door.

Then it came.

She watched the fingers bunch up at the end of an arm drawn back with the jerky motion of Charlie Chaplin in one of the old reruns on late night TV; she watched the arm stop beside Hank's head and float there, dark hairs streaking the fingers below knuckles white with anger and desire, then move toward her lips, the same lips Hank liked to kiss when he danced slow with her at Club Harem just south of Amarillo, his hands locked behind her back, one thumb hooked over her belt so she felt his fingers brushing the tightness of her jeans. The fist came as in slow motion, and Drusilla wondered at herself for thinking of dancing and of kissing Hank even as he swung a fist toward her mouth.

Her knees gave with fear, and she slid down against the door. Hank's fist slammed into the door, through it, into something inside that exploded glassy and sharp. He screamed.

She scrambled out of the way, stood, watched as Hank struggled to extricate his hand from the shattered wood, from the wire rack he himself had attached to the inside of the pantry door. He lurched this way and that, looking at her, his eyes smoky with desire to hurt, but the hand remained caught. He kicked the door. "Lookit what you made me do, you stupid girl." The words came out low, dangerous, and he stopped struggling for a moment to examine the problem of his fist stuck in the door.

Drusilla looked at the Frydaddy. The potatoes sizzled in golden perfection, exactly as Hank had taught her to cook them. She looked at Hank. Blood ran down his wrist, circled his arm, dripped. "I'll kill you for this."

The first time he had struck her, he called it a spanking. She needed it, he explained, for her sloppiness in the kitchen, she needed to be turned over his knees, to have her skirt pulled up and her panties down so he could pop her bare bottom. She had laughed and squirmed, figuring he was joking, and her laughter enraged him into a low growl with each blow to her bottom. Later, after he became contrite and they made love, she was sure he had meant the spanking as a joke until she laughed. She told him she was sorry she had made him mad.

The next time, he blackened her cheek below one eye. He cried when he saw it, later, after the smoky burning went from his eyes, he cried, and she found herself comforting him. Drusilla, with a stinging cheek bruised black, took his hand and kissed it, telling him she was sorry.

When she thought about it later, when she stood before the mirror in the bathroom and looked at the dark swelling, she wondered at herself, at how she could let him strike her with those sledgehammer fists, then comfort him in his guilt, even allow him to kiss her, to love her on the floor of the living room, not three feet from where he had made his fingers into an ugly ball to slam into her face.

The attacks came with greater frequency, and each time he grew quiet afterward, grew heavy with guilt and shame, and expected her to minister to him, expected her to make love.

But he had never told her he would kill her.

Drusilla picked up the snapping Frydaddy and emptied the grease in a quick pitch, aiming for the back of Hank's head. He turned as she jerked the pot toward him.

A golden tongue of oil licked his face with a sizzle. Blobs of it landed on his shoulder and chest in a wet slap. He howled and jerked free from the door.

Drusilla moved to the arch separating kitchen from den, watching him dance around the kitchen. He breathed out in jerks, saying, "ah, ah, ah, ah," in a quick rhythm, moving much as he did for a fast dance at Club Harem, his grunting sounds coming out as a parody of the jerky way he laughed when amused. Drusilla listened and watched his macabre co-ordination of sound and movement, his feet shuffling in a puddle of oil on the linoleum, and she thought of laughter, grotesque grunts of laughter syncopated to the rhythm of each step in his hot-oil dance.

Blood dripped from the hand he wrenched from the door, and slices of golden potatoes clung to his shirt and hair. One eye lolled hideous and ruined, the other flashed this way and that, a part of the insane ballet through the oil, his uninjured hand flailing about, fingers touching face, head, chest.

Hank slipped, crashed against the Frydaddy on the floor, scrambled to his feet and slapped the faucets in the sink into producing a silver stream, bubbly with a sound like frying. He splashed water into his face, into the ruined eye, and he howled again.

Drusilla took a step back into the den when she heard Hank's "ah, an, ah" turn into a word: "kill, kill, kill." She looked around, feeling the terror rise within her. A cloisonne vase sat on the mantle above the fireplace, a vase that had been a gift on their honeymoon.

She found it in a little shop along the river walk in San Antonio, admired the butterflies and flowers on it, and Hank had bought it for her. The vase was his first and only gift.

Set into what had been a bookcase beside the fireplace were Hank's guns, locked behind a glass door. "Not guns," he told her once, his voice dripping with contempt for her stupidity. "Pistols. Rifles. There isn't a single shotgun in there. Guns." He had shaken his head as at a child.

Hank kept the key to the case in his pocket, forbade her ever to touch the weapons, ten of them, sleek and ugly, stinking of oil when he handled them. His favorite was a pistol, one he loved taking to the couch to snap open and finger the bullets. Then he clicked it closed and cocked it: snick-snick it said, oily in metallic precision. He liked aiming it at her. "Never point this at anyone," he liked to say. "It has a hair trigger when it's cocked like this." Then he'd release the hammer, using both hands, sliding it into its deadly place. Snick-snick.

Drusilla picked up the cloisonne vase, looked at the butterflies, thought of the day on the river walk when he bought it for her, looked at the ceramic flowers edged with brass.

She smashed the vase into the door of the gun case, smashed again and again until she could lift out the pistol. When she turned, she found Hank standing in the arch between kitchen and den, looking at her with a single eye, burning and wild. "Gimme that pistol."

She backed toward the hall leading to the front door. He stumbled into the den. "Gimme that." Oil dripped on the carpet from his shirt, and blood ran from the fingers he had bunched together when he burned to strike her lips; blood ran in crooked lines from wrist to fingertips, falling to dark spots on the carpet, and for a moment she wondered how to clean the stains: with cold water, maybe, and Degreaser? Then she laughed aloud at herself. Her voice startled her for the note of hysteria in it. She saw Hank stiffen at the sound of laughter.

He stumbled toward the gun cabinet muttering, "Ah, ah, ah, ah."

Drusilla looked down the long hallway from the den to the front door, to the light coming through the glass, to the shadows cast by an afternoon sun—shadows in the crooked shape of the firethorn bush growing as an arch above the entry. She looked at Hank.

He fumbled in the cabinet with his good hand, scratching a blood line on it from a shard of glass, pulled out a rifle; he muttered in a rhythmic pattern and lurched right and left in what struck Drusilla as an effort to stay on his feet.

Could I kill him? she wondered and looked at the ugly pistol, felt its oil on her palm, smelled the sharpness of it, thought she could not, thought it better to leave.

It seemed to take hours to get through the hallway to the front door, to open it in a blinding stab of sun, to force herself out of the house beneath the firethorn arch of leaves, thorns, and blood-red berries. The automatic sprinkler system had just started to glisten the lawn. Her feet struck a puddled sidewalk with dull plops, like a palm slapping wet flesh. She couldn't breathe, couldn't breathe. Then she heard him, stopped, turned on the sidewalk, looked back.

Hank stood in the doorway, unsteady and struggling with the rifle. He cradled it in his bloody arm while doing something to the bolt with his good hand. The flush across his ruined face and eye reminded Drusilla of the flush that came upon him when he stiffened at the height of passion. A slice of potato glinted golden in his hair, catching a beam of sun through the firethorn arbor. He snapped the bolt into place and began to lift the rifle.

Drusilla looked at the pistol. Can I do it? she asked again, her hands coming up in front of her. When she fingered the mechanism, she heard its oily sound. Snick-snick.

The pistol jumped in her hand, then jumped again and again, making a sharp cracking sound, rhythmic and flat, much like the sound her feet had made on the wet sidewalk. She inhaled with a quick snatch of air, desperate for breath as if she had been long under water, and she felt hot tears on her cheeks.

Brother Jones and the Snake

Rosa stood among peonies, among gladiolus, poppies, pansies, among hibiscus, called *bunga raya* or the king of flowers by Malays, the irrelevant memory of the term coming to me through a mist of anger. She stood in the still air moist from the river and from the arrival of wet season and heavy with the nectar of flowers Rochelle liked to tend, heavy with perfume from jungle flowers, especially the frangipani blossoms in a tree towering over the bamboo wall, odors to cloy with too much sweetness in the wet air. I glanced at Rosa's unbuttoned blouse and her tee shirt untucked in front and remembered what Brother Jones had said about offering her an entertainment and about sending me a gift so I would get something out of the deal. The unbuttoning and untucking had to be part of his notion of entertainment.

For an instant Rosa had a strawberry on her neck; she wore fake buckskins and beads of another woman who once betrayed me, one I married, but the instant came fast and went fast leaving no strawberry, only the worried face of Rosa who might or might not have enjoyed Brother Jones' notion of entertainment. Certainly I hated what I got from his deal, hated finding in my room a child who thought she had to submit to adult abuse, hated Brother Jones for sending her, hated him enough to go after him with a machete as I once went after Phung Phuoc with a sharpened bit of bamboo, hated enough to thrust Rochelle into Rosa's care, Rosa's unbuttoned blouse making my head light with anger to multiply hatred enough to look for the false shepherd beyond the garden gate until Rosa called out to show me the unlocked jungle gate where Brother Jones fled after his entertainment, fled to seek his God in a jungle he figured was the devil's dominion, though of course he knew nothing about the jungle as a true place of evil, knew nothing about Vietnam where a tiger could come for you in the night and the likes of Phung Phuoc cut rattan for beating American prisoners. I hated with the same cold fury that drove me to kneel beside the sleeping Phuoc and raise the stake, double-handed, its point black from the black earth.

"The pistol," Rosa called in warning, and I saw it black against Jim's white pants, his white shirt, saw it as I first did when he came to the boat dock—when? that morning? Was it just hours ago that Rosa and I docked our canoe at the edge of the compound and first saw Brother Jones— and now I planned his death, if you can call cold fury planning, saw the pistol or a bit of it under the leather covering and shook my head to fling away the vision. I went through the open gate, beneath frangipani blossoms, in a run to make the canteen bounce against my hip, heading toward the tree riddled with insect holes where I knew I'd find the man who sent a child—a member of his own flock—into my bedroom in exchange for Rosa, and I heard his words, "I have devised an entertainment for her," too pompous and absurd for me to consider any seriousness of intent on his part, heard my own voice in compliance without suspecting his dark design.

I heard him in the woods ahead and ducked, circled to watch for an opening so I could rush him before he unsnapped the pistol, heard his cry of alarm, heard him struggle. I moved faster, arm crooked and machete up, ready to strike and aware in a faint way of sweat sticky between my fingers. Then I saw him.

It must have dropped on him from a tree, and it pinned his arms to his sides. The snake's mouth clung to Brother Jones' face, the top teeth holding just above one ear and the bottom gripping his jaw, and Brother Jones struggled to get a hand to his pistol, had unsnapped the covering of the holster but could do no more because of the coils pinning his arms. The flare of its jaws, the size of it, the terrifying power of it stopped me for an instant, and I saw another snake in another jungle flare its neck, arch back and launch venom to glisten in a shaft of light, its spray aimed at Allen's eyes as he turned toward it, not knowing of its presence beside him where he sat, waiting for me, and I might have shot the snake before it spat its poison, but I didn't, I didn't. The memory of my failure unfroze my legs, and I ran to Brother Jones, slipped the machete over his shoulder, beneath the python and drew the blade toward me with outward pressure to slice into the snake below its open mouth. The snake writhed and I felt water hitting me and thought it must be rain gathering in the jungle canopy to fall in such large drops, and I sliced again and the snake writhed with the slicing, then became still and Brother Jones had the pistol out but with the wrong hand and not gripped for firing so it was easy to take it from him to drop it to the ground and begin prying the snake's head from Brother Jones' face. He fell to his knees. I kicked the pistol away, fearful he would pick it up, put it to his head, a fear that didn't make any sense, not there in the terrible jungle outside the compound on the river, and I knelt beside him, ignoring his muttering, finding it necessary to lift the jaws, finding the snake's teeth curved inward for the lock on the head it tried to swallow. When the snake gave up its grip on Brother Jones' face and hit the ground, it moved as if to crawl away though I had thought it dead; it turned as if to escape into the jungle, and I snatched up the machete and chopped at its head, at the bloody place where the machete had bit into it, chopped again and again yelling "Die you damn cobra, die, die," until the head lay apart from the body, the huge body that continued to quiver while Brother Jones staggered to his pistol, then stood over the severed head to point and make the pistol pop and put a hole near the python's nose.

"That was no cobra." His voice carried scorn for me perhaps or perhaps for the dead snake that wasn't a cobra, and he fell again to his knees to mutter more words.

Only then could I stand still, could I realize the water I felt was snake blood that spurted my arms and chest, my pants and shoes—on my hands even, sticky and familiar on my hands in a way that send a shiver of horror through me; but Brother Jones had more on him, crimson thick and darker than human blood, though some of that also trickled down his face from the stitching of teeth punctures. Snake blood covered his shoulder, his back and chest in fluid almost too thick to drip.

The cold fury had abated to leave me trembling and on the edge of being dizzy with the same spinning that got me after using the bamboo stake on Phung Phuoc. It wasn't until I had put the machete handle under my belt that I realized Brother Jones wore no shirt, that he was still partly dressed for the entertainment he devised for Rosa, and the realization brought again a wave of fury, a small wave that came and went while I fumbled with the lid to the canteen to splash water on my hands for wiping the sticky off on the back of my pants. I commanded myself to listen to his words.

". . . for the snake and for deliverance from the snake, Lord, I thank Thee, and for this unholy baptism to show me thy covenant and let me know Thy time is at hand. I thank Thee for Tom and his righteous blade, for—"

"Can the crap, Jones," I said. "I didn't come here to save you from a python. I came to kill you for, for . . ." I faltered. For what? Getting into Rosa's pants? Prostituting a little girl? I wiped my hands again.

"No, my friend. You came here to do what you did." He dropped the pistol into his holster and picked up the snake's head. "Satan, I fear thee no longer."

"It's only a snake, damn it. A python. It felt your motion and figured you were a rabbit or an armadillo, and it released its grip on the tree hoping to fall on its lunch. If it had known how large an animal you are, it would have stayed in the tree."

"Thanks for the scientific explanation. You are, of course, wrong. But no matter. Believe what you want. I thought you might be the sign, then believed it to be Rosa with her dark eyes and beauty to disguise corruption. She had to be it, and I came into this fallen garden not knowing her to be a mere catalyst, that I would find the Prince of Darkness here as the sign, the final sign. You and I and Rosa are now bound by this blood. You are part of the covenant." He stood, cast down the python's head and stepped on it.

I followed him toward the compound. It took all my energy to hold back the dizziness, to keep from seeing the cobra lifting itself in front of Allen, and I knew I was stunned by the fury that had dragged me into the jungle to kill Brother Jones, stunned by the killing of the python and the way my fury had vanished, stunned by the feeling of blood making my hands sticky. I wondered if I could take the machete and hack into Brother Jones right there beneath the canopy of trees not unlike those Phuoc slept under when I got him with the sharpened bamboo, and I imagined doing it. I could grip the machete, take three quick steps, and sink it at an angle into his neck. His own blood, a lighter red, would gush over the thicker, darker snake blood and he would stagger and I would feel the quiver of his death throes through my grip on the machete as if it were a spear of bamboo, and he would half turn to look at me with yellow eyes, eyes whose light faded even as he buckled to his knees. Could I do that?

The amazing thing to me wasn't that such an act seemed impossible but that it had been possible before the python fell on him, that only moments before I could have killed in hot blood. Then what? Then he would come to me in odd moments as Phuoc came to me, as my wife came to me with the strawberry of infidelity on her neck though I didn't kill her, wouldn't under any circumstances kill her and yet I was a killer of men and worse, much worse than other soldiers who seemed to learn something from what they did in Vietnam while I didn't learn from what I did to Phuoc with the sharpened bamboo; I didn't learn a thing or it would have been impossible to thrust Rochelle into Rosa's care and go after Brother Jones, to stalk him, to watch for an opening so I could rush in to chop the machete into him before he could draw the pistol. Killer, killer, killer they said to me when I came back to the States, the landlady said that when she asked if I was a vet and I said yes and she said to go away, that she didn't rent to killers so I had to learn not to confess to being a vet or else listen to their abuse and feel their anger making what I had done in those evil jungles even worse than it had been before listening to their taunts, worse because I believed them and hated myself for being a killer, killer, killer. But that was in war, I argued again and again and perhaps came to believe the excuse though here in this jungle there was no war and yet I had the machete in hand with the same intent that I once gripped my rifle, the same intent that drove me to kneel over a sleeping man and raise the sharpened bamboo above his neck.

We reached the compound. Brother Jones went to the Commons, to the bell suspended above a cement block where he had placed the jar of arsenic. He picked up a piece of rebar iron to ring the bell and I wandered toward the flowers hoping to find Rosa, needing the comfort of her presence even if she might be a woman who could succumb to the charms of Brother Jones, a man she disliked at first sight and yet unbuttoned for when he took her to his siesta room. No matter, I told myself. No matter. She didn't go after Brother Jones with a machete. She is better than I, far better.

Freshwater Pearl

Billy Ray Redmon watched Norma Jean nearly turn the canoe over as she climbed in, and he took her awkwardness as evidence confirming what he already knew: that she couldn't possibly be his soul mate.

He glanced toward the sun and calculated they had three hours of canoeing before they had to find a place to camp for the night.

Though he liked Norma Jean, he knew their relationship was doomed to be a brief one. For one thing, there was her red shoulder bag, no doubt filled with the self-indulgent powders and perfumes of a female narcissist. Also he had learned the day before that she wasn't a Texan, that she grew up in Phoenix, and was thus a big city girl who no doubt hated rural places, especially in Texas.

He pushed the canoe into the river and climbed in, for he was determined to enjoy two days on the Brazos River, and especially two nights of camping in the same tent with Norma Jean. Or he would enjoy the nights, if he could convince her to do more than sleep beside him.

"I'm confused," Norma Jean said.

"Join the club," he muttered.

"I read the book, *Goodbye to a River*, as you suggested. But the river's still here. Possum Kingdom Dam didn't destroy the river. And the water is so clear. It's beautiful. I love it here."

He didn't expect such enthusiasm from her. As she turned in the canoe to look at him, he feared he would see pouty lips in spite of her words. She smiled.

"I've wondered the same thing when I first saw the river from the highway," he admitted. "I've tried fishing under the bridge, but I had no luck. Maybe our canoe trip will tell us why John Graves thought the river was forever gone."

She picked up her paddle. "I'll have to learn to use this thing properly," she said.

"I told you I would do all the work. You don't need to paddle."

111

He thought of how Olympia had refused to do anything that might make her sweat, even stroll around his family's ranch. "We could look for arrowheads," he said with enthusiasm as he drove Olympia toward the ranch. She had laughed at the suggestion, laughed in a mean way.

"I think I understand the physics of it," Norma Jean said. "I paddle on one side just to help push us along, and in the back you steer the canoe while you paddle. Right?"

"Yes. Excellent." He felt pleased, and he tried to remind himself that Norma Jean Collins wasn't the same lady as Olympia Flanders.

"Wait, wait." Norma spoke in hushed tones. "Is that a great blue heron?" She pointed.

"Yes. One of my favorite birds."

"Don't paddle. Give me a minute." She fumbled with the red bag she had flung into the canoe before she had almost tipped it over.

Billy Ray watched in astonishment as she took out a camera.

Olympia had responded much differently when she saw a beautiful bird. And it wasn't just any bird.

They had been on the dirt road leading to his parents' ranch when he spotted the painted bunting, stopped the car and rolled down the windows.

"You're letting dust in." Olympia's voice sounded dangerously close to a whine.

"There," he pointed, "That bird in the low mesquite. Do you see it?" She glanced toward the bird. "So?"

"It might be the most beautiful bird in Texas. Look at those brilliant blues and reds. It's as if a third-grader with a perfect sense of color painted it."

Olympia stared at him. "It's a bird. It's just a bird," she had said.

When they resumed paddling, a headwind slowed their progress. If they stopped pushing so hard, the headwind blew them back upriver. "This is discouraging," Billy said. "There's not enough flow to help us move along, and this stiff headwind makes us work even harder."

"The exercise will be good for us, then," Norma Jean said.

After about an hour of paddling, Billy brought the canoe close to a sign at the edge of the water.

Norma Jean read the sign aloud, her voice filled with outrage. "'Coming on this property isn't worth getting shot.' Who would put up such a terrible sign?"

"A crotchety old rancher, maybe," Billy said. "Someone who has had to put up with people leaving trash on his land."

"Do some ranchers in Texas think littering is an offence that should carry the death penalty?"

"No, no. It's just Texas exaggeration. That rancher wouldn't shoot anyone."

"Then let's go ashore." Her voice carried a teasing tone.

"No way." Billy paddled the canoe back into what should be the main current, though he found the river barely moved.

Norma Jean turned to look at him in amusement. Or he thought it was amusement. Maybe it was triumph? He shrugged and decided that he resented her challenging him to go ashore, and such a mean-spirited challenge was reason enough for his working so hard to seduce her. He had to admit, though, that the expression on her face hadn't been all that mean—maybe not mean at all.

Olympia Flanders had not put on her mean face until the first morning when they awakened at his parent's ranch. She shrieked when she found a scorpion in the bathtub. "That's it," she declared. "We're leaving."

"Over a scorpion?" Billy had muttered, and he chose to ignore her outburst.

I should have expected her insulting comments that morning about the baby goat, Billy thought as he pushed the canoe around a bend in the river. Why didn't I?

Even as he asked, he knew the answer. It had to do with the terrific sex there in the bedroom that had been his while growing up. I was blinded by her beauty and addled by her prowess in bed, he thought.

But that won't happen with Norma Jean, he decided, who just happens to be as pretty as Olympia. Prettier, even. But then, how could he be addled by Norma Jean's sexuality? She refused to make love with him, though she did so in a sweet way. Three dates and still no sex. But that could have been okay with him since what he wanted went way beyond sex.

He wanted a soul mate. But Norma Jean had struck out in that department, so he had given up on anything profound with her, and having sex became his main goal for the camping trip.

Maybe tonight? After all, she knows we'll be sleeping in the same small tent. Billy felt his pulse quicken at the possibility. He leaned over the side to admire the clarity of the water and some clam shells on the bottom. They shimmered in mother-of-pearl.

"An eagle," Norma Jean pointed. "A bald eagle. Wow."

The huge bird swept close to the water. Billy loved the majesty of the eagle. Again he remembered his disappointment when Olympia dismissed the painted bunting as just a bird.

The canoe hit a rock and spun around. Billy wasn't sure of what happened next. Did he stand up to dislodge the bow from the rock? Did Norma Jean lean too far to one side? One thing was sure: the canoe flipped, and Billy went under water, though when he stood he found that the river at that point was only waist deep. He grabbed the canoe, turned it over, and began pushing it toward the bank. Norma seemed to be splashing around, no doubt in a helpless flutter like Olympia had been over the scorpion. He ignored her, concentrating on getting the boat ashore and emptied of water. When he turned back to the river, he saw Norma Jean dragging in the cooler.

Just a few yards away, stacked in a neat pile sat the contents of the canoe: his duffle bags, the paddles, her red bag, and a soaked wicker basket. "You rescued everything?" he asked in astonishment.

"Nearly. The basket of food is empty. Everything in it simply vanished."

He nodded. Maybe he had misjudged her. Maybe she could after all become more than a brief entertainment, though he didn't hold much hope for it. "I thought you told me you couldn't swim."

"I never said that. Besides, the river is shallow enough to wade across. And there isn't much current, so it was easy to catch all the gear."

"We might as well camp here. There's a flat place right up there where we can pitch the tent."

"Among all the wine cups and Indian blankets? Wow."

Her response pleased him. Not only did she like some of his favorite birds and wildflowers, but she knew the names of them—unlike Olympia, beautiful and sexy Olympia who so hated his family's ranch in West Texas.

The sealed duffle bags kept their contents dry, so Billy had no problems setting up camp, though he found a small rip in the nylon close to the top of the tent. "Not good." He glanced at the sky. "But I checked the weather before we came. It isn't supposed to rain."

"I might help with that." Norma Jean took something out of her red bag.

"Duct tape," he said in astonishment. "You brought duct tape."

"Sure, why not? It's great for patching lots of things. Here." She pulled off a strip of the tape, bit into it so she could tear it from the roll, then sealed the rip in the top of the nylon tent. Billy watched in amazement.

When he put the air mattress into tent and hooked up the motor to inflate it, Norma Jean knelt beside him to watch. "You brought air mattresses?" she asked in surprise.

"Mattress. Just one. But it's large. A queen-sized one. It will barely fit in the tent."

"I hope you didn't have any plans about using that mattress for anything but sleep," she said.

Billy winced but tried to hide his response. "No. No plans."

Why couldn't she be more like Olympia? he asked himself, a woman who had jumped his bones on the night of their first date. And the energy Olympia put into the act began his desire for her to be his soul mate.

"I thought not," Norma Jean said. "But you realize, of course, that most guys would believe that taking me camping for two nights would mean making out in a tent. I'm glad you're not like most guys."

He turned away so she couldn't see his burning cheeks, cleared his throat, and waved a hand toward the empty wicker basket. "We're out of luck for dinner. I've got some bacon and some sausage in the cooler, but the skillet was in the basket, so it's gone, and now we don't have a way to cook."

Norma dimpled in what he took to be amusement. "There's always a way to do what you need to do. We're clever people, and we have the river as a resource. We won't go hungry. Did you see all those huge clam shells along the edge of the river? That means there's live ones to be found. Come on."

So this lady will go clam hunting in the muck of river sand, Billy thought, and Olympia wouldn't even go hunting for arrowheads on the hardscrabble of his parents' ranch.

After she seemed to recover from her snit over the scorpion in the tub, Olympia irritated Billy at breakfast by making a big deal over biting into a bit of eggshell in the scrambled eggs. Billy's mom, her cheeks red from the insult, took away Olympia's plate with an apology and brought in another, this one piled high with French toast and honey. Olympia had pushed the plate away from her.

As he waded into the Brazos with Norma, he realized he should have known in that moment of the insult to his mother that Olympia couldn't be the person he should marry.

Norma picked up a flat rock to use for digging in the sand. "Here," she said with triumph. "A nice one. How many would make a meal?" She tossed the clam to Billy.

It felt heavy and was huge, larger than his fist. "I thought you said you had never been on a river."

"No. I said I had never canoed a river. Here's another one. As you might guess, I have had some experience digging clams. But I was looking for freshwater pearls, not for a meal."

"Do you know how to cook clams?"

Norma glanced at him, frowned as in thought and chewed her lip. "No. But I'll bet we can come up with something."

Olympia couldn't cook at all, Billy remembered. "Nor do I want to learn," she told him over breakfast that day on the ranch, the day he had foolishly set aside to propose marriage. "If I tried even boiling water, I would likely scorch it." And she laughed at her own cleverness.

"I can tell you're a big city girl," Billy's father said. "I'll bet you've never seen a baby goat."

Earlier, the old man had talked to Billy about introducing Olympia to his baby goats, for he was certain she would be charmed by them. "There's hardly any critter in the world as cute as a baby goat," he told Olympia. "Adults are a mite troublesome, but you need to see a baby."

"No I don't," Olympia said. "I want nothing to do with smelly animals."

His father winced and fell silent, and Billy had felt a stab in his chest, a pain that warned him of great loss.

After Billy found a clam and Norma dug several more, she set them on the bank, took off her blouse, and tied it into a pouch for carrying the clams. Billy stared in surprise.

"Stop that," she said. "My bra covers me as well as would any bathing suit."

"Sorry," Billy mumbled.

"You're so cute with your wonderful old fashioned ways." Norma Jean laughed.

As they walked back to the camp, she said, "It would be a good idea to gather some firewood."

"Uh-oh," Billy said. "The matches. They were in that wicker basket. They'll be either soaked or on the bottom of the river."

"Wet matches? Let's gather the wood anyway. Over there." She pointed. "There's a pile of driftwood."

When he neared the tent with an armload of wood, he found Norma digging through her red bag, no doubt, he thought, for something frivolous or frilly.

Billy hated that red bag. It looked almost exactly like the one Olympia took to the ranch, a bag full of what he considered ultra feminine junk: makeup, perfumes, soaps and lotions. Not that he hated everything in the bag, and especially not the lotion after Olympia had asked him to rub it on her wonderful body. It smelled like peaches.

That day at the ranch he came to despise the bag because it seemed to epitomize Olympia's self-absorbed and mean-spirited nature, especially what he saw in her as she packed the red bag, slamming her junk into it with such fury on her face. "I'll not stay on this ranch," she declared. "You will drive me back to Austin. Now."

To Billy 's amazement, Norma Jean pulled a compass out of her red bag, not a frilly bottle of any sort. She held the compass over a pile of twigs and leaves she had gathered, and it was only with the twigs began to smoke that Billy realized the compass was set on a base that also held a magnifying glass.

"I borrowed a spark from the sun to light our dinner fire," she said.

Poetry, Billy thought, she spoke pure poetry. And though he liked poetry, he distrusted it. Hadn't Olympia liked poetry? Seems like she was all the time quoting some old dead guy she called Edgar Guest, and they were poems Billy didn't like much.

Still, Billy mused, maybe I need to rethink my reason for this canoe trip. His dating her hadn't started with a plan for sexual seduction.

The courtship of Norma Jean was born of wild pain, the deep sense of loss he felt when he realized Olympia could not possibly be the soul mate and wife he so longed for. Even before Olympia shouldered her red bag and headed down the dirt road where, she said, she would thumb down a ride back to Austin, Billy's dad had put his hand on Billy's shoulder and said, "Son, that gal is big city born and raised, and you might need to forgive her for that."

It took a week of reading postings on the web dating service for Billy to find Norma Jean. It was her double first name that caught his eye. Billy figured only rural Texans liked to hang such names on their children, and he wanted to meet a rural Texas woman.

Olympia had presented herself as being a country girl, as liking to camp, to hike, to fish. But she lied. It took Billy what he knew to be longer than reasonable to catch on to her lies, and when he saw that fury on her face, that meanness in her stomping out of the house and down the road, red bag on her shoulder, he wondered if all women were such fakes. Duplicitous. No damned good.

He meant to break up with Olympia as soon as he got back to Austin, but she beat him to the punch. She did it with a letter, an unkind one. It began with proclaiming herself to be a Yankee, a New York city girl who had gone to some public school with a number instead of a name. She said she had no explanation for her lying about loving the outdoors and the rustic life. That's when Billy swore he would never again fall for someone from a big city.

When he saw her name on the dating service, he felt certain that Norma Jean Collins had to be a proper country girl. So he contacted her, set up a meeting, and the two agreed on a date. Billy expected her to drag him into bed that very night, as Olympia had done on their first date, and when Norma Jean made it clear that he wasn't invited into her home at the end of the date, he was so delighted that he didn't even try to kiss her, though she had clearly expected him to try.

"Maybe," Billy said, "we can put the clams into the fire and roast them."

"That might work. If they start popping open, we could rake them out to see if they're cooked enough."

To Norma Jean's surprise, or so she said, the meal was a huge success, for she loved the clams. Billy agreed, though he thought the chewing proved to be more work than fun—and he disliked the bit of sand grit in each bite. Norma Jean didn't mention the gritty texture at all, much to Billy's delight.

That night in the tent, Billy said, "I'll stay way over here on this side, okay?" He hoped she would say no, come closer.

"I knew you would say something like that. You are such a good man, Billy Redmon. I doubt you even know how many points you score with me by being so sweet and so moral."

Damn, Billy thought.

The next morning Billy and Norma rekindled the campfire. At Norma's request, he whittled several pointed sticks that she used for skewering and roasting some of the bacon from the cooler.

The river continued to offer headwind and little current. They paddled through a deep place, then over shallow rocks to another deep place. Then the canoe struck round stones in shallow water. "We need to drag the canoe," Billy said. He climbed out and picked up a clam shell to admire the rainbows in it. "Did you ever find one?"

"Find one what?" Norma Jean asked.

"A freshwater pearl."

"Maybe." She laughed, and Billy wondered what she found amusing.

As they pushed the canoe into deep water, she said, "This river isn't exactly a river. It's more like a necklace. The little ponds are like the pearls, and they're connected by bits of shallow, rocky water. The Brazos isn't a river any more. It's a series of ponds or little lakes. Graves was right to say goodbye to the river."

More poetry, Billy thought with both pleasure and some discomfort.

By noon he began to worry about what they would find for lunch. He did have, tucked into his waterproof duffle bag, a spinning reel attached to a telescoping rod. And he had hooks and some lures, but he doubted he could catch anything. His last attempt when he fished under the highway bridge had resulted only in snagging some brush.

Then he saw the catfish line. One end was secured to a willow, and the tug on the other end told him that the line had caught a fish. "There's our next meal." He took the canoe to the line.

"No," Norma Jean said. "That's not ours. Someone else set that line."

"The person who put out this line doesn't know about the fish or he would have taken it off the hook. Besides, I doubt any fisherman would begrudge us a meal, if he knew our circumstances." Billy pulled up the line and lifted a fish into the canoe. "A yellow catfish. Good eating."

"We don't have to steal the fish." Norma Jean took his reel and telescoping rod from the duffle bag. "I saw this rig when you set up camp last night. Maybe I can use it to catch us a fish for lunch."

"A bird in hand." Billy nodded toward the catfish by his feet. "It isn't easy to catch fish in most Texas rivers."

With a sigh, Norma Jean set aside the fishing gear and opened the cooler. "If we're going to steal that fish, the least we can do is to rebait the hook. Hand me that line."

"You're serious?" Billy put his boot on the catfish and extracted the hook from its mouth. He handed the line to Norma.

With a few expert-looking twists, she threaded a slice of bacon on the hook, then dropped the line into the water. Billy stared in open admiration.

Around the next bend in the river, he nosed the canoe into a sandbar, a high one, flat on the top, a place that held an abundance of dried driftwood. As they pulled the canoe ashore, Norma Jean asked, "Would you like me to clean the fish?"

He thought she was joking. "Sure. I'll gather firewood." He grinned.

But his grin vanished when she took a substantial-looking hunting knife from her red bag.

119

"No, wait," he said. "I'll clean the catfish. It's messy, and it's not woman's work."

"Don't fillet it, then. Just gut it and wash it out. That way it'll be easier to roast. I'll build a fire."

That evening, Billy enjoyed a second fish meal with Norma Jean. She had caught a bass, one he estimated to be eighteen inches long. As she had done for lunch, Norma Jean smoked the fish on a crude but effective rotisserie.

"There's no fences here," Norma said as they buried the trash from their meal. "And look—that dirt road runs into some trees. Let's explore the area."

"You want to go for a walk on a ranch?" Billy looked at her in amazement and admiration.

In the woods they found a cemetery, an old one surrounded by a fallen-down fence of rusted barbed wire. Norma Jean walked around, reading inscriptions on tombstones. "This is wonderful," she said. "But what's a burial ground doing out here, in the middle of nowhere?"

"In Texas," Billy said, "you can have a private cemetery if you own at least a hundred acres. Or so my father says. We have a place like this on our family land near Brady."

"I would love to see that ranch," Norma Jean said. "What's this at the base of this stone?" She bent for a closer look. "A brass plaque someone added recently. And the top part of the tombstone has broken away. There it is on the ground."

"What does the plaque say?"

"'Citizen of the Republic of Texas,'" Norma read. "The stone says her name was Elizabeth. Help me pick up the broken part of the headstone and put it back together."

Billy picked up the stone and tried to set it in place. "It'll fall as soon as I let it go."

"Then we need to fix it." Norma chewed her lip. "Find a tree limb three or four inches thick and about the height of the tombstone. I'll be right back."

Billy watched her step over the fallen fence and head toward their camp.

He kicked around under the sycamore trees at the edge of the cemetery until he found a suitable stick.

When Norma Jean returned carrying her roll of duct tape, she told Billy to put the broken tombstone back together and to stand the stick behind the pieces. She taped the stones to the piece of wood, then taped the brass plaque to the base of the headstone.

"That's better." Norma Jean stood before the repaired stone and held out a hand to Billy .

"It's a temporary fix." He took her hand. "It won't last long."

"Everything is temporary," Norma Jean said. "Some things are just more temporary than others."

On their walk back to the river, Billy said, "I'm glad you put Elizabeth's headstone back together." He meant to add 'and I love you for it,' but he managed to get out only, "and I love you" before the words seemed to grow thick and lodge in his throat.

Norma Jean laughed in genuine amusement.

He glanced at her, unsure of the meaning in the laugh, and he felt his ears grow hot, for he had not meant to blurt out that last part. He spoke fast to cover his embarrassment: "I would have sworn that only a Texan would think to repair a tombstone with duct tape."

At dusk, Norma Jean took a bar of soap from her red bag. "I want to bathe in that wonderful river." She glanced at him. "You, too. Come on."

He followed her to the water and watched in astonishment as she dropped her clothes on a rock and waded into the water.

"This is handmade soap." She held up the bar. "It smells divine. Come on. I'll share." She dived into the water, then stood to rub her hair into creamy lather.

When he joined her, he tried not to look at Norma Jean, though in that moment he knew her to be the most beautiful creature in the world.

"Here." She handed him the soap. "And thank you for not staring."

When they returned to the riverbank, he wrapped his shirt around his waist and walked ahead of her to avoid the temptation to stare. Inside the tent he put on clean underwear and a tee shirt, and he took his place on the far side of the air mattress. She entered the tent in a nightgown and startled him by coming to his side, almost touching.

"You're the most genuine gentleman I've ever met," she whispered. "If you want, I'm now willing to make love."

"I do want that. More than you know. But not tonight. Maybe a kiss. That would be perfect. He leaned toward her, taking care to touch only in a brushing of lips. "Do you believe it's possible for people to be soul mates?"

She retreated to the other edge of the mattress. "Wow. Soul mates. And that chaste kiss. Amazing. A huge surprise. You're such a romantic."

"Is that bad?" he asked.

"Being a romantic? No. Not bad. Good, maybe. You continue to astound me. My guess is that right now you're about to ask me to marry you."

Billy felt his heart beating hard, fast, and his face flush. He tried to find the right words.

"Don't do that," Norma Jean said. "Don't propose to me."

Billy felt himself spinning, dropping somehow, and he again felt the stab of loss in his chest, the same kind of pain that hit him as he watched Olympia walk away from the ranch, the same as he felt reading her final letter, especially the part about her being a proper city girl and his being a simple country bumpkin.

"At least," Norma Jean added, "not yet. Don't propose yet, okay?"

"Okay." The pain left him, and he stared at the dark strip of duct tape that held together the rip in the top of the tent.

Hard Scrabble Jury

"Justice demands that we hang these two fellers." Dorf Jolson paused for a dramatic sneer at the two boys. He glanced toward the burning clouds on the horizon and thought it best to hurry the trial. Fun or no fun, the jury would soon revert to rowdy cowboys hollering at One-Eyed Boyle to serve up the beans and biscuits, such as they were. Boyle made the hardest, nastiest biscuits of any chuck wagon cook west of Palo Duro Canyon.

"They ain't fellers," a member of the jury said. "They's boys."

"They chose to come into the world of hard knocks, so I say we don't cut them no slack for being boys," another jury member said. A chorus of voices added "yeah," and "get a rope," and many of them chuckled in a mean way. One held up a noose.

"Judge Boyle," Dorf Jolson said, "please tell the jury to bite their tongues and listen."

"Do it." One-Eyed Boyle kicked a clump of buffalo grass to emphasize his statement. "Do what dwarf Jolson says."

"Dorf, dangit. Dorf Jolson."

"If he was a dwarf I'd wrestle him to the dirt and stuff his mouth full of goat-headed burrs," the smaller of the two boys said. The larger one whimpered and smeared a tear across his cheek. "And you quit that blubbering." The smaller one shoved his companion.

"That Samuel kid's feisty as a banny rooster," a member of the jury said.

"Stole a mule, that's what Samuel and his buddy done," Dorf Jolson said, "and everbody knows stealing a mule is almost the same as stealing a horse."

"Hang um," the jury member said.

"Do it." One-Eyed Boyle kicked the clump of buffalo grass again, put a finger to his lips and pointed at the jury in a fierce way. "Do it."

The larger boy let out a wail and Samuel punched his arm. "He ain't saying to hang us, not yet, anyway. He's telling them to shut their mouths. It ain't time for the sentencing, so you quit being such a bawl bag."

"You boys. You do it too." One-eyed Boyle stamped his boot in their direction.

The older boy sniffed and made an effort to stop crying. The jury muttered, settling on the prairie hard scrabble, and fell into silence punctuated by some elbowing and subdued laughter.

"Broke their mama's hearts is what they done, running away from home like that." Dorf Jolson puffed his chest and looked outraged. "Took off from school at recess and went straight for Jimmy Joe's Livery on Polk Street, they did, and no bothering to say adios or nothing to them that was raising them. Stole that mule and headed west where I caught them crossing the Frying Pan."

"If we hadn't of took it, that mule would be dead," Samuel said. "Jimmy Joe was about to take that mule out to Horse Head Lake and shoot it on account of being old and stubborn. It ain't stealing to take a mule that's about to get shot."

"These here boys," Dorf Jolson said, "are a bad sort. I've known nicer boys than these to drag the family wash in the mud, to put a lump of tar in the teacher's chair, and even to chunk a dirt clod in the butter churn."

"We ain't never done such," Samuel said. "Never."

"So I say we find them guilty of breaking their mamas' hearts and of stealing a mule, and we sentence them to hang."

"Hang um, hang um," the jury said.

"That all?" One-Eyed Boyle asked. "If so, then the jury has spoken. Hanging it is."

"What about a last meal?" one member of the jury asked. "Least we could do is give them some of One-Eyed Boyle's biscuits."

The jury laughed and Dorf Jolson struggled to keep a straight face. "It would take them boys all night and well into morning to chew biscuits hard as them rocks One-Eyed Boyle cooks. We got no time for such a last meal, so I say we hang them."

"You dad-burned ungrateful cowboys," One-Eyed Boyle said. "Ain't nothing wrong with my biscuits."

"That's true," Dorf Jolson said, "long as you're using them for driving nails or for fishing sinkers."

"I got something to say," Samuel struggled to his feet in spite of being hobbled. The older boy glanced up an Samuel, covered his face with his hands and sobbed. "You shut up," Samuel said through clenched teeth.

"And you fellers ain't the law. You're just a bunch of Frying Pan Ranch cowpokes, everbody knows that. You ain't the law so it ain't legal for you to hang nobody."

"It's legal," Dorf Jolson said. "Texas law number five seven nine was introduced in the Austin state house by Noah Webster and Alexander Hamilton and it passed last year. As of this year it's legal for men working on ranches out west to set up juries and hang them that needs hanging, and breaking a mama's heart is a hanging offense in West Texas."

"Hang um, hang um," the jury chanted.

"I ain't got no mama," Samuel said. "Back in Amarillo I got only uncle Shadrach Reed, and he woulda helped me run away if he'd seen me doing it."

"Don't matter none," One-Eyed Boyle said. "Who got the nooses?"

"You cowboys is mule stubborn and skunk stupid." Samuel glared around him. "Get on with it, then."

The older boy sobbed louder than ever. Jury members crowded around the boys to watch the nooses snugged up to their necks, and even Samuel teared up, though he tried to hide it.

"Problem is," Dorf Jolson said, "the nearest tree is a stand of cottonwoods bout eight miles away. I ain't up to riding that far before supper. I say we stop the hanging and sentence these boys to going home to Amarillo. They gotta take the mule back to the livery, of course."

"Hang um," some of the jury members said, and others said, "send um home."

"Cut um loose," One-Eyed Boyle said.

"Bring the mule," Dorf Jolson said.

"I ain't going," Samuel said. "You just got to hang me."

"Can't," Dorf Jolson said. "We done changed the sentence and it ain't legal to hang you, not now. You gotta go home."

"Hire me on, then." Samuel snatched the noose as one of the cowboys tried to take it from his neck. "Hire me or take me to the cottonwoods and hang me."

"I want to go home," the older boy said. One of the cowboys untied his ankles and helped him get on the mule.

"You can make it to Polk Street by dark," Dorf Jolson said. "You, too, Samuel. Get on the mule."

Samuel held up the rope with the noose on his neck and turned around as if he were hanging from a tree and twisting in the wind. "I'll hang before going back."

"You don't know nothing about cows." Dorf Jolson said. "You ain't worth nothing to us."

"I can help the cook, then. My uncle Shadrach weren't much, but he did teach me how to make sourdough biscuits."

The cowboys became stone silent, then one of them slapped the mule's rump. "Get on back to Amarillo," he said. "Get, now." The mule headed east with the older boy urging it on.

"Sourdough biscuits," Dorf Jolson said in amazement. "A boy that can make biscuits."

"I don't need no nasty little boy telling me how to be a cook," One-Eyed Boyle said.

"The hell you don't," Dorf Jolson said. "What do you say, boys? Do we hire Samuel or hang him."

"Hire him, hire him," the jury chanted.

Samuel pulled the rope from his neck and threw it on the ground. "You bunch of stupid cowpokes," he said.

Canoeing the Hill Country

Leaning Bear read the sign on the bridge, "Colorado River," and he thought about a saying his father liked to repeat: "names determine destiny."

"So," Leaning Bear turned to the passenger side of the pickup as if his father were sitting there, "the river will be red because of its name, right?" In the middle of the bridge he stopped the pickup, got out, opened the topper on the bed of the truck and dropped the tailgate. He blinked hard at the sting of tears. Ducking under the canoe strapped on top of the pickup, he took out a golf bag and heaved it over the bridge railing. "Goodbye, Dad," he said. "Dead or not, you're once again lord of the waters."

The golf bag floated for mere seconds before the current wrapped it in rust-colored water and tugged it under. He knew the river would pull, bit by bit, the ashes of his father from where he had poured them into the ball pocket on the side of the bag. "And take your holy seat." He jerked out and tossed into the river the green plastic chair his father had used for patio-sitting, for watching the river by day. At night the old man sat in the chair to watch for falling stars.

"There'll be none tonight." Leaning Bear glanced at the heavy clouds, then looked at the river for the chair. It had already vanished.

"But of course the stars are always there, clouds or no," his father said.

With a shake of the head, Leaning Bear affirmed that he would not talk to Varun, not right then when there was the canoe to launch.

Light rain spotted the windshield as he got into the cab of the pickup. By the time he crossed the bridge and found the dirt road leading back to the river, it had begun to rain in earnest. "This is foolish," his father said, "running the river with night coming. Besides, I keep telling you that you're not the kind of Indian to ride in a canoe."

"You won't make this any easier for me, will you?" Leaning Bear coughed to cover a sob, for he feared hearing his father's laughter.

But Varun laughed anyway. He sounded loud and mean and fully present.

Don't talk to him, Leaning Bear told himself. Talk to someone else, anyone else. He parked beside pillars holding up the bridge. "Mom?" he said. But she wouldn't answer, as usual.

He knew his dad was right, that a flash flood could wash him away while he slept. Why, his mother would demand—if she were still speaking to him—are you taking this dangerous journey?

"I don't know," he said. "But I am. It seems right that today of all days I ride the river through the Hill Country."

It took only minutes to set the canoe on wet grass and load it with a cooler, his tent, and waterproof bags of camping supplies. He eyed the space left in the canoe and decided he didn't have room for his folding camp chair. "Bummer," he said and locked the pickup. Only then did he scout out the riverbank for a place to launch. It didn't look good.

"That's a forty-five degree incline," Varun said.

"Please, Dad, be quiet and tend to your final business as Varun." Leaning Bear dragged the canoe across wet grass and across low mounds where the skidding energized fire ants. At the edge of the incline he looped the aftline around a tree and looked down at the reddish water.

"You're brave," Varun said. "And you know the bravery comes from your true name. Abhay means—"

"Brave. As if you need to keep telling me that. Please remember the so-called family name is something you hung on us. I got into many fights for having the name *booze shit*."

"Bhooshit, and say it right, *Bahoo-zit*. It means—"

"Mom," Leaning Bear said, "you like me as Leaning Bear." He pushed the canoe down the incline and caught its sliding fall with the rope on the tree. Talking to Mom often stopped the old man's lectures.

The canoe launched well enough, and the rope held it to the bank. "New rule, everyone," he said as he stepped into the canoe. "Nobody but me gets to speak while I'm on this river."

Frankie said, "dat's crappo," and Portia said, "I'll talk when I damn well please," and Varun said, "You'll get me talking soon enough."

As the rain turned into a mist, a feral hog swam the river ahead of his canoe. Leaning Bear felt mild alarm at the size of the creature, at the way it turned to eye him when it climbed up the bank. "Is that contempt I see in your eyes?" he asked the hog.

"No," the hog said. "Try to remember what Winston Churchill said about dogs, cats, and hogs."

"Amusing," Leaning Bear told the hog. "That's amusing." He tried to conjure a memory of what Churchill wrote: "Dogs worship us, cats ignore us, and pigs have contempt for us." Or something like that, Leaning Bear thought. "Pigs," he told the hog. "Churchill used the word *pigs* not *hogs*."

The feral hog snorted and vanished into the underbrush, and Leaning Bear felt the bank had become a place of danger. Didn't wild hogs sometimes attack people? Best not to camp near there, he thought.

The river widened and the first rock cliff of the Hill Country appeared, a craggy presence lined with desert varnish and speckled with yellow cactus blossoms, some of them already closing for the night. Across the main channel from the cliff a sandbar jutted from the water.

He nosed the canoe into the shallows, dragged it onto the lower part of the sandbar, and carried all supplies to an area where grasses and weeds suggested flood waters had not reached for months. After setting up the tent, he knelt inside to connect a battery-driven pump to his air mattress. "Would a real Indian sleep on an air mattress?" he asked.

"Better a bed of nails," Varun said.

"Yeah, right. Like the one you never used, not even in India during your hippy days."

"Your bed of nails," Varun said, "was with your wife. Do you know the origin of her name, Portia?"

"Dad, isn't it time for you to leave?"

With the coming of twilight, the misting rain stopped, and Leaning Bear looked around for firewood. The river had pushed an abundance of dead branches and other trash into a tree on the end of the sandbar. "Too wet," Leaning Bear said. He rummaged through the pile, pulled out a green plastic chair, and examined it with elaborate care. "I didn't need your chair, Dad," he said.

"But you left yours." Varun's voice had a mocking tone—or maybe, Leaning Bear thought, simply an amused tone.

Leaning Bear set the chair beside the tent, took a sandwich and a Bavarian-style ale from the cooler, and sat down. The clouds had drifted into small clumps, revealing a clean array of stars that astonished Leaning Bear.

"I told you," Varun said.

"What? Not gone yet? Why are you here, anyway?"

"Why are you?" Varun laughed.

When the time came for him to go into the tent for the night, Leaning Bear asked himself why indeed he was there. He turned his attention to the white-noise gurgle of the river and drifted into sleep. At what point the river became a different one, he could not say. He knew it to be the Bhagmati, a muddy stream winding its way through Katmandu and past the cremation stones of Pashupatina Temple. Smoke came from a pyre below where he and his father watched from a stone railing. The man tending the pyre used a staff to rake something oily-looking from the fire, then pounded the object with fury. "That's the oldest son tending the funeral fire of his father," Varun said. "It's the son's duty. When the fire has consumed the body, its ashes will be swept into the river."

The calm voice of his father frightened Leaning Bear, as did the white smoke and the burnt meat smell in the air. In a shifting that he thought should have surprised him but did not, he felt the staff in his hands, and he knew the smoky object he pounded with the staff was his father's lungs, a knowledge that stung his eyes worse than did the smoke. The lungs are the hardest to burn, someone had told him.

"Rake them back into the fire," Varun said. "We must utterly destroy the body, for the soul will linger beside it in confusion instead of moving on to another life."

The man tending the pyre raked the black lump into the fire, and Leaning Bear felt a stabbing pain in his chest when the fire started on his lungs. "Not yet," he said. "Not yet, not yet."

He awoke with a start and a sharp pinch of angina as he listened to the sound of the Bhagmati. "No," he said, speaking to the darkness. "Not the Bhagmati. This is the Colorado River in the Texas Hill Country," and images from the dream drifted into a memory of being a child and watching a Nepalese ceremony of cremation with his father many years before.

With a flashlight in hand, he got out of the tent and examined the river. It ran lower than it did when there was daylight. He returned to the air mattress and slept with only vague and spongy dreams.

Morning twilight came with the river releasing bits of itself in wisps of fog, with the splash of fish gar, with a river otter surfacing to make eye contact with Leaning Bear. It disconcerted him to discover the river had fallen in the night so that his island had become a sandbar peninsula. That meant more work in loading and launching the canoe.

Then he saw the golf bag jammed into sand where the night before a finger of the river flowed through a shallow channel. He descended the bank, prodded the golf bag with a toe, and asked, "Why are you here?"

"I found the camping spot for you," Varun said. "I waited."

"You did not. And you have not been reborn as a golf bag, Varun." Leaning Bear pulled the bag from the sand, turned it so he could unsnap the pocket designed for golf balls, and he felt inside. "Grit." He looked at his fingers. "And some ashes. I had hoped for better." He dragged the golf bag up the bank, across his campsite, and shoved the bag into the river.

Later, as he canoed past cliffs rife with mud bottle swallows, he asked, "How did the golf bag get there?"

"I threw it in the river," Frankie said.

"You did no such thing."

"But I did." Frankie sounded affronted. "Why do you think they call me Frankie the Snake?"

"Dad called you that because of your beady eyes."

"Dats more of your crappo. It's because I like to steal, even from family. Your nutty dad invited me to his place, and when I got there I found this wreath on the door. The old goat had died, it seems. It was easy work to jimmy a window. I took his antique coins, the ones from India and Nepal. And I took the golf bag, then decided it wasn't worth hocking, so I parked on the Highway 16 bridge and threw it into the Colorado."

Leaning Bear stopped paddling to watch swallows pecking in the clay at the base of a cliff. He liked how they fluttered about, hauling bits of mud for building nests to help their babies grow strong so they could make mud nests for their own young before the coming of death. And so the birds go on forever, Leaning Bear thought. In that moment he decided he hated talking to Frankie. "You'd tell a lie with the truth sounded better," he said. "And you named yourself Frankie the Snake."

"Maybe I added the snake part," Frankie said. "But I was born your daddy's nephew and named Frankie, just like you were born Abby Hay Bullshit."

"Abhay. My name was Abhay, but I wasn't born with it. My hippy father hung that name on me after Mom died and after he and I went to Nepal and India. He found our new names in Jaipur. The family name he gave us was pronounced—"

"Whatever. You named yourself Leaning Bear so you wouldn't have to be Abby Hay bullshit."

"If you were here," Leaning Bear said, "I'd toss you out of the canoe."

"Your dad was a fungus-headed moron."

Leaning Bear felt a flash of anger. "Shut up, Frankie."

"Frankie the Snake lives up to his name," Varun said.

"I thought by now you would be gone into the waters of the holy river," Leaning Bear said.

"Remember those guys in Amarillo named Boxwell? Do you think it accidental they opened a funeral home? And that hospital in Dallas, you remember how I said only a dope would go to a place called Deadman Hospital?"

"D-e-d-man," Leaning Bear said. "Not dead man."

"What will the name *Leaning* get you? And what use is it to be named after a bear? There are no wild bears left in Texas."

"The name has made my life peaceful."

"Why did you choose an American Indian name?"

"I've got the dark eyes and hair for it, and the good brown skin. So why not? You chose Indian names for us when I was a little kid."

"India Indian. I found real Indian names, ones that shaped our lives."

"It was your shape, not mine. Your shape was wrong for me. Dad, you need to move on, and if you insist on hanging around, then at least stop talking to me."

"You have it wrong. I'm trying to go, but you won't release me."

"I'm holding on to nothing." Leaning Bear blinked back tears and resumed paddling. That evening he made camp on a low sandbar that looked to be a permanent island, for the river split around it with deep water on both sides.

In the morning he sat on a rock to watch the river at the point where it divided to flow around his island. A spot of sun upriver set the water to glowing, and fog patches clung to the water. "Beautiful," Leaning Bear said.

"Peaceful," Varun said. "It was this very spot where Siddhartha sat for years to learn from the river and to contemplate the nature of enlightenment."

"This is the Colorado, Dad. This is Texas and not India."

"India, Nepal, Texas," Varun said. "Tell me Abhay, what is the difference when it comes to a peaceful river and enlightenment?"

"You're lecturing me again. I don't believe in any of your goofy ideas, and please remember my name is Leaning Bear, not Abby Hay Bullshit."

"That's your cousin Frankie talking, not you. Stop listening to Frankie."

Somehow the charm fled that Leaning Bear had seen in the early morning river, and he struggled to resist a profound sadness that threatened to settle into the core of his being.

As he broke camp, Portia said, "Don't you dare leave that beer bottle or any other trash on this island."

"I don't litter," Leaning Bear said. "You never bothered to learn that, did you? You nagged me every day of our married life. Pick up this. Clean up that. Your fingernails are dirty and want trimming. You're wearing the wrong shirt. Those shoes are a scandal. Your belt is too wide. Your tie is too narrow."

"I was not nagging. I was telling the truth." Portia sounded defensive.

"Your truth. Not mine."

"You have too many truths, and they all contradict. But do you know what I hated most about you?"

"I'm sure you are about to tell me. It might be better, though, for you to say nothing."

"What really drove me nuts was your constant talk. You wouldn't talk to me, hell no. But no matter what you were doing, you kept up a running monologue. You talked to yourself, and that's almost crazy. Then you answered yourself, and that is for a fact crazy. I left you because you are crazy."

"Tell her what her name means," Varun said.

"You tell her, Dad."

"There you go," Portia said, "Talking to your dad again, and he's not even here."

"He said Portia comes from Latin *porcius*, meaning pig." Leaning Bear smiled, toothy and mean. She fell silent, as he expected, but he knew she wouldn't be quiet long.

He collapsed the tent, folded it, picked up the ale bottle and put it into his growing bag of trash. "You told me you left because I changed my name."

"That, too," Portia said. "Remember back in college before we married, you emailed me that you were a bit depressed and found yourself leaning at odd angles? I thought what you said was clever and poetic. I should never have told you that, because you took it as permission to change your name to one you thought was clever and poetic. *Leaning Bear*, what a stupid and embarrassing name, especially when you told our friends. How they laughed behind your back. I was so humiliated."

"Must everything be about you? I'll let you talk to me one more time, and that's it. Forever."

When Leaning Bear got the canoe back on the river, he felt out of sorts, and he found little joy in paddling, though the river offered some class two rapids that would, on normal days, be great fun to ride.

"This is hardly a normal day," Varun said.

"A railroad trestle." Leaning Bear pointed. He felt a bit foolish for the gesture and hoped no one saw. A quick glance on both sides of the river assured him he was still far from any people. Then he saw the truck on the bridge. It was outfitted with railroad wheels, and it had stopped over the water. As Leaning Bear drew closer, the pickup door opened and a man leaned out, cupped his hands around his mouth, and asked,

"Are you catching any fish?"

There's actually a man up there talking to me, Leaning Bear thought. A real person. "No luck today," he said. "The water's too muddy for catching bass."

"You're not fishing for bass," Varun said. "You aren't fishing at all."

"Please, Dad, be quiet" Leaning Bear muttered so the man on the bridge wouldn't hear.

"You're careful now," Portia said, "but you didn't care at all if my friends heard you talking to yourself like a crazy man."

"That's it for you, Portia." Leaning Bear kept his voice low.

"Good luck," the man in the pickup said.

In less than a mile the canoe went under another bridge. "That has to be Highway 190," Leaning Bear said.

"Right you are," Frankie said. "Have you seen the golf bag again?"

When he paddled into some rapids, Leaning Bear misread them, and he felt the bottom of the canoe scrape on rocks. The water spun him sideways, and he paddled hard to keep from turning over. A sudden surge of current pushed him into a channel near the bank, and a dead tree poked a finger above the canoe to scratch his ribs. He shoved hard with the paddle against the snag to get the canoe back in the rushing water.

"Class three white water, and I ran it," he said with enthusiasm, pumped his fist and raised his voice to a loud "Yes, yes!"

His voice startled a bald eagle. It flapped out of a cottonwood tree and circled over the canoe. That critter looks cross and out of sorts, Leaning Bear thought.

"What are you doing here?" the eagle demanded.

"I don't know," Leaning Bear said.

"You're not an Indian," the eagle said.

"No, and this isn't India."

"That's not what the eagle meant," Frankie said.

What a silly and obnoxious man Frankie has become, Leaning Bear told himself. I'm finished with him.

"India. Texas." Varun said. "It makes no difference in the great scheme of things."

Later in the day when Leaning Bear calculated that he was likely approaching Colorado Bend State Park, he came to a wide spot in the river where there was no channel, and white water rushed over rocks from one bank to another. Five young men played in the rapids. "Shallow water," Leaning Bear muttered.

The canoe hit a rock and flipped over. Current slammed his leg against a bolder. He struggled to his feet, grabbed the aft rope as it swirled by, and braced himself to stop the canoe from washing away. His ice chest, the bag that held his tent, and his waterproof bags bobbed away in the current. As he steadied the canoe, he became aware that the men playing in the rapids were catching some of his gear.

When he got the canoe to the bank, he turned it to empty the water and dragged the boat onto shore. "I caught one of your paddles," one fellow said.

Another waded ashore, waterproof bag in tow. "Thanks," Leaning Bear said, though what the man had rescued contained only his camp garbage.

A third man came ashore pulling the ice chest. Its lid flapped this way and that, and it contained only water. "Sorry I couldn't catch any of the bottles and other stuff," the man said. He wore cutoff jeans and a tee-shirt. "I'm Owen Netter." He gestured at the other men, who had all returned to the river. "Those are my brothers."

"Leaning Bear." He held out his hand to Owen. "You're kidding me that you are all named Netter, right?"

Owen smiled. "You mean because we netted your camping gear? We do get kidded much about our names."

"Looks like," Leaning Bear said, "I lost my tent and air mattress. I'll be bedding down on the ground tonight, just me and the dirt and the stars. But that's okay. Does much junk float past this spot in the river?"

"Some." Owen jerked a thumb to point behind him. "There's something I caught this morning in the rapids. No kidding. Some golfer must have lost it."

Startled, Leaning Bear looked at his father's golf bag. "Was there any sand or ashes in it?"

"Ashes?" Owen looked perplexed. "Nah. Just the bag, clean as a whistle. Not even any sand caught in the pockets —I guess the stiff current cleaned it out. And I love to golf. What a gift from the water, right?"

"That's great. I'm more delighted than you could know." Leaning Bear tried to keep his voice from breaking with emotion.

Another young man came ashore, and Owen said, "That's my brother Osburne. Osburne, this is Leaning Bear."

"Wow," Osburne said. "An Indian. Is that why you're canoeing the river?"

"Is it, Varun?" Leaning Bear muttered, hoping Varun couldn't talk.

"What's that?" Osburne asked.

"I said you asked a good question." Leaning Bear tried for a smile. "My guess is that I'm canoeing the river to run away from being an Indian."

He heard Varun's laughter, a gentle and loving sound this time. It was loud at first, then faded with distance to vanish into the roar of river water tumbling over rocks.

Leaning Bear sighed with relief and rubbed his eyes.

Brenda without Skin

Kent Day first noticed Noland Fritch in the Dallas International airport while boarding a flight to Denver. And in Denver, he saw Noland get on the same plane he did for Seattle. It wasn't hard to notice Noland because of his height, exaggerated by a white Stetson, and what Kent regarded as his almost comical western dress. He wore light blue, brushed cotton jeans; lizard cowboy boots; a hand-tooled belt that said NOLAND FRITCH across the back and had a four-inch buckle in front; a tight red-and-blue shirt with pearl-covered snaps instead of buttons, and flaps over the pockets; and a string tie clasp with a scorpion enclosed in clear plastic.

On the flight to Denver, Kent took out his sketch pad and a box of pastel chalk. He drew Noland in caricature, making the figure stoop to keep from bumping his head on the ceiling of the plane. Beside him, Kent put a stewardess looking up at him in awe, her chin brushing Noland's gigantic belt buckle. He drew Noland's legs toothpick thin, his hips almost non-existent, and his shoulders impossibly broad. On Noland's handsome, square-jawed face, Kent drew a confused, stupid look. Why am I doing this, Kent wondered, even as he began shading the absurd cowboy clothing in the very colors Noland was wearing. Why caricature someone who is already a caricature?

When the woman sitting next to Kent said, "That is terrific," Kent began to regret doing the drawing. "You are a real artist," the woman said. "Would you do one of me? I would buy it from you, of course."

Kent flushed crimson and closed his sketch pad. Being a commercial artist was, he wanted to believe, a thing of his past. He had worked as artist-in-residence for two years at the Hotel Galvez in Galveston, drawing caricatures of the tourists and charging a fat enough fee to be able to bank the money he needed to go to art school to learn to be a real artist. Even while studying at The University of Houston, he returned to Galveston during the summers to do his time as a hack so that, one day, he could put

137

what he regarded as crass commercial art behind him. When the day arrived—when he managed to be among the first in an artists' exchange program between Selangor in Malaysia and the state of Texas, what do I do? he asked himself. I go back to mucking around in caricature work, that's what. He shook his head.

There were other heads from the past shaking, looking with disapproval at him. The one Kent was most aware of wore the garb of a Roman Catholic nun. Sister Corazon. Kent felt certain that she would have scorned his work at the Hotel Galvez.

He had been in East Texas, at Jefferson City shopping Center in Port Arthur, doing several days in a starving artist show, making not much at all, when, out of frustration over nobody noticing him, he began singing "Your Cheating Heart" as loud as he could. People up and down the sidewalk stopped to stare. "Who's the nut?" they wanted to know, and grinning faces crowded around. Before long, he was doing a booming business in caricatures, and he jacked his prices up a few bucks. When the crowd around him thinned, he broke into song again, singing whatever came to mind: "Does Your Chewing Gum Lose its Flavor on the Bedpost Over Night?" and other odd-ball classics of the Texas hit parade from years ago. He knew he couldn't sing worth a damn, but he was loud, not at all self conscious, and outrageous enough to draw plenty of attention. The crowd loved him. A man from the *Port Arthur News* took his photograph, and an article appeared in the paper the next morning about the singing artist. That day, the manager of the Hotel Galvez became one of his customers, and by the next day, Kent was packing up to move to Galveston to become artist in residence at the hotel, though not without feeling guilty about it.

The guilt aside, it was a good life, Kent reflected, living at the hotel and making big bucks, by a young artist's standards. But it wasn't what he wanted, and he knew one day he would abandon such commercialism forever. And yet here he was, twenty thousand feet over the Rocky Mountains, blasting that poor cowboy in coarse, commercial form just to amuse himself, and there was the woman next to him, the epitome of all the wealthy tourists who wandered through Hotel Galvez, offering money for his services as commercial artist. He looked again at the woman beside him. Fortyish, he decided, quite beautiful, aware of her appeal to men and used to it. He glanced at her tight pants, her stylish blouse that revealed a slight bit of cleavage. Oil money, maybe, or cattle dollars bought that outfit, he thought. She looked as if she just stepped out of Neiman Marcus.

"I'll do a drawing of you," he said, "but only under the condition that you pay no more than you think it's worth and that you not pay anything at all if you don't like it."

She protested, flashing charm, sexuality, and a smile that revealed the expensive, subtle wiring Kent had seen before in mid-life orthodontics. He insisted on his terms. "Don't look until it's finished."

Kent put away the pastels and got out a black pen. He would do her in ink, he decided, with care and with real artistry. And just maybe a little meanness for her catching him at the piece of fluff he zapped Noland with. He had her sit on the aisle seat, leaving an empty one between them so he could turn and look at her with more ease. Then he drew her as if she were sitting in the plane with not one scrap of clothes on.

Doing the piece reminded Kent of all those nights he studied Brenda Watson through the window of the house next door. Almost every night she undressed and paraded around her room, lights on and curtains open, and he sat just feet away in the darkness of his room, feeling the juices flow with vigor through his thirteen-year-old body, telling himself that he was making a study of anatomy for drawing later that night. As soon as she turned out her lights, Kent turned his on and got out the special sketch pad he kept under his chest of drawers. "Fantasy Girl" he had labeled the pad, just in case anyone ever found it and wondered who the model was. Not that anyone would wonder. He was always careful to put Marilyn Monroe's face on the body.

He wasn't that good at drawing the body, though certain parts he did an outstanding job with. One day, on impulse, he showed the pad to Esmund Drakes, a new kid in school he wanted to be friends with, a kid who could draw comic strip characters with amazing speed and accuracy. Kent didn't tell about the nighttime modeling sessions, though. He would just as soon Esmund think the girl was supposed to be Marilyn Monroe. Esmund was so impressed that, when he left Kent's home, he sneaked out with Kent's sketch pad tucked inside his own.

The next day, Esmund took Kent's drawings of Brenda to school and handed them out to various guys in the cafeteria. Marilyn-Brenda, the fantasy girl Kent had kept such a secret for so long, created a sensation, and before he knew what was going on, boys were coming up to Kent, asking for more such drawings. At one table, a scuffle broke out between Haines Cunningham and Jim Hudson, a couple of the school's track stars, over ownership of a drawing. "Lookit them tits," Haines said. Jim tried to look, but Haines held the drawing away, repeating, "Wouldja just lookit them tits." Jim made a snatch for the drawing, and Haines punched his arm. Other guys gathered around the table, gawking and pushing each other to get a look. The activity caught the attention of Sister Charlotte—Sherman Tank Charlotte, the kids called her. Guys scattered at her approach, all but Jim Hudson and Haines Cunningham, who had their backs to her and were too involved in their contest over the drawing to notice much of anything.

Kent watched in agony as Sherman Tank Charlotte's eyes went round and her puffy lips formed a huge O, making her face, encircled by the nun's habit, look like a gigantic circle with three smaller circles drawn inside, the three connected by a banana that was her nose. Kent sketched the face on his napkin even as Sister Charlotte grabbed up Jim Hudson and Haines Cunningham by their collars. She lifted them from their chairs and banged their bodies together before dropping them in a confused heap in front of her. "Hand me that trash," she said in the high, fluting voice that she used in moments of great distress, "and you two come with me."

The rest of the afternoon proved to be one of the longest of Kent's life. He expected to be called to the main office to talk with the new principal, Sister Corazon, who had come to Bishop Green Intermediate School with the reputation of being a tough lady to deal with. But the summons did not come.

That night, he watched Brenda with less than his usual enthusiasm, and afterward he found he could not draw a thing. During second period the following day the summons came.

Sherman Tank Charlotte herself delivered the message to Kent, and as he left math class to follow her down the hall, he heard uneasy laughter from some of the guys in the class.

The hallway felt longer, narrower, and darker than Kent remembered it. He noticed some cobwebs near the ceiling, and in a couple of places the dark, excremental flecks of chewing tobacco that some of the guys dropped on the floor while scooping out a jaw full of Bull Durham. This is it, he thought. Endsville. He got a vision of Sister Charlotte tying a blindfold over his eyes while Sister Corazon lined up a firing squad, headed by Esmund Drakes and Brenda Watson. "Do you want a final chew of tobacco before the execution?" Sherman Tank Charlotte asked.

"I don't chew," Kent said.

"What was that?" Sister Charlotte held the door to the principal's office open.

Kent looked at her with alarmed confusion. "Uh, after you." Kent felt dizzy.

"Stuff the charm." She scowled. "Nothing can save you now."

He knew that was true, but to hear it from Sister Charlotte made his knees turn to jelly. As he walked in, Esmund hurried out, his eyes downcast. Kent thought Esmund looked much like his dog did when it got caught piddling on the floor. Sister Charlotte gestured into the private office of the principal and gave Kent a shove in that direction.

He looked around the room in a panic. No windows. And the only door was behind him, blocked by a Sherman tank. He took a deep breath and let himself into the principal's office.

Sister Corazon stood by a window, the backlight ringing her so it was impossible for Kent to make out her facial features. Except for being smaller, she might have been Sister Charlotte standing there. "Please sit down, Kent Day." She indicated a chair in front of her desk, then walked to her chair and sat, looking at Kent in a most disconcerting and steady way.

Kent met her gaze, something he had taught himself to do with people when he decided he wanted to learn to draw faces. But holding eye contact with Sister Corazon was tough.

"You realize, of course, that you have committed a number of offenses?" She picked up a stack of his drawings and dropped them a little closer to him on her desk. "Do you?"

"Do I what?" Kent asked, then realized what she meant and stammered, "Yes, uh, yes I did. Do."

"The human body," she held eye contact as if she were challenging him to be the first to look away, "is the temple of the soul. You realize that, of course?"

He said nothing. It seemed to him as if she had penned him down with her steady gaze.

"You have tried to draw that divine temple in a rather poor way. Marilyn Monroe once was a real, live, breathing human being, but no more. Now she is a myth, an unreal entity, a chimera, a kind of dream that people try to give substance to in their dreams. You tried that, and you failed. Miserably. Do you understand what I have said?"

"No."

"That, at least is honest. This," she broke eye contact for the first time, and Kent felt as if someone had just taken a knife from his throat. "This," she picked up the drawings of Marilyn-Brenda, "is bad on a number of counts. It isn't a good rendering of the myth. It concentrates on making a woman's body something it is not, on making it into a thing, an object. And remember that a body is holy. Always remember that." She walked to the trash can and dropped the drawings into it, then stood for a few seconds, looking at the contents of the can.

She turned to Kent. "The first offense was drawing without working out what the body looks like. You brought talent to the task, along with ignorance." She went to a bookcase, removed a book, and opened it on her desk. "Come look at this."

Kent stood with uncertainty and looked at the book. It was some sort of anatomy text, and the picture she had opened to showed a human body with no skin in order to illustrate the shapes of the body's muscles.

"That is part of the foundation." Sister Corazon pointed. "This one is female. On the next page is the male."

Kent turned a page, caught by the lines of muscles wrapping the body. He picked the book up and turned another page, then looked up, embarrassed.

"Would you like to borrow the book?"

At that point he understood what Sister Corazon was up to.

Kent looked at various parts of the woman's anatomy as she sat in the airplane seat, fidgeting, unsure of how to respond to the intensity and frankness of the way he looked at her. He thought of the shape of her body, only partly hidden by her clothing, of the smooth flow of muscles under her skin, and moved his pen with precision. She was beautiful, and his pen celebrated her beauty. Sister Corazon, could she see the drawing, would approve, for he was drawing the beauty of this woman, and was catching something of her tentative, nervous and yet self confident personality. A human being, Kent knew. Alive, beautiful, perhaps aging a bit, but not an object.

His next attempt to draw Brenda, which came just days after the interview with Sister Corazon, showed her in profile, standing beside a bed, wearing no clothes. In this drawing Brenda wore no skin. "She is beautiful," Sister Corazon said when she looked at the drawing. Even the facial muscles were there, wrapping the jaw and encasing the eyeball. Some of the perspectives were not quite right. Her head was too small, and her pectorals too large.

At the principal's suggestion, he drew skeletons, working on getting the dimensions of the various bones the proper size in relationship to each other. At night he studied Brenda, then drew her bones in the various positions he saw her take in her room: sitting before the mirror, combing non-existent hair with skeletal fingers grasping a comb; lying on the bed, reading through empty sockets; standing with one bony finger poised over the light switch. Watching her and seeing bones and muscles and light and shading became exercises in self control and objectivity. He never told Sister Corazon about his model, even when he showed her drawings of Brenda wrapped in flesh and wearing the self-satisfied, flirtatious and naughty grin she often had when glancing in the direction of his darkened window. Sister Corazon always approved, for he was learning, and he was being honest.

"You have great talent," she told him once. "Use it for creating truth and beauty. Never be dishonest as an artist." Was drawing caricatures being dishonest? He wasn't sure, but suspected it was at least doing less than he should be doing, less than he was capable of. But there was the persistent need for money, and caricatures brought plenty of that.

Kent completed the drawing of the nude lady. It would be easy to drape her in clothes, but to alter the drawing at this point would do bad things to it. He knew the piece was as good as anything he had done lately, yet he wasn't pleased with it. He handed her the drawing with much the same feeling he used to have when showing Sister Corazon a new drawing of Brenda. Then he remembered his original motives for striping his subject of clothing. A mean-spirited motive. Kent blushed, ashamed to have allowed himself to act on such a base feeling.

The woman looked at the drawing, then at Kent. "This is wonderful," she said. "Don't be embarrassed over it."

Kent made no attempt to correct her analysis of his blush. He watched her study the drawing.

"You captured some things about me that not many people know." She moved into the seat next to him again. "I've posed nude for other artists, but you did a better job than any of them, and I was fully dressed." There was awe in her voice. "Would you please sign the drawing?"

As the two parted in the Denver airport, the woman handed him a folded hundred dollar bill, blushing as she did so. Her awkwardness made Kent feel awkward, though he was quite used to people handing him money for his work. The woman hurried off, and Kent looked at the bill she had given him, realizing that there was another hundred wrapped inside it.

He wadded up the bills and jammed them into a pocket, glad to have the money and at the same time disappointed and more than a bit angry at himself.

Other Books from Mongrel Empire Press

Alan Berecka, *Remembering the Body*
Joey Brown, *Oklahomaography*
Nathan Brown, *My Sideways Heart*
Nathan Brown, *Not Exactly Job*
Robert Murray Davis, *Born Again Skeptic & Other Valedictions*
Jim Drummond, *The Coyotes Forgive You*
Duane Hada and Ken Hada, *The River White, A Confluence of Brush & Quill*
Ken Hada, *Spare Parts*
Catherine L. Hobbs, Ed, *Are You Doing Fine, Oklahoma?*
Kathleen Johnson, *Subterranean Red*
JLC Mish, Ed, *Ain't Nobody That Can Sing Like Me, New Oklahoma Writing: Poetry, Fiction, Creative Nonfiction*
Joe Dale Nevaquaya, *Leaving Holes & Selected New Writings*
Judith Tate O'Brien, *Crossing A Different Bridge*
Patrick Ocampo, *Surface Tension Poetry & Flash Fiction*
John G. Rodwan, Jr., *Fighters & Writers*
Alvin O. Turner, *Hanging Men, Poems based on the 1909 Ada Vigilante Hangings*
Alvin O. Turner, *L.W. Marks, A Baptist Progressive in Missouri & Oklahoma*
Anca Vlasopolos, *Walking Toward Solstice*
Jerry Wilson, *Blackjacks & Blue Devils*

Find out more about these books:
www.mongrelempire.org

www.ingramcontent.com/pod-product-compliance
Lightning Source LLC
Chambersburg PA
CBHW020643250626
47154CB00008B/2788